Cici #2
A Fairy's Tale
~ TRUTH IN SIGHT ~

Written by
Cori Doerrfeld

Illustrated by
Tyler Page and Cori Doerrfeld

GRAPHIC UNIVERSE™ · MINNEAPOLIS

Graphic Universe™
A division of Lerner Publishing Group, Inc.
241 First Avenue North
Minneapolis, MN 55401 USA

For reading levels and more information, look up this title at www.lernerbooks.com.

Main body text set in CCDaveGibbonsLower 10/11.
Typeface provided by ComicCraft.

Library of Congress Cataloging-in-Publication Data

Names: Doerrfeld, Cori, author, illustrator. I Page, Tyler, 1976- illustrator.
Title: Truth in sight / written by Cori Doerrfeld ; illustrated by Tyler Page and Cori
    Doerrfeld.
Description: Minneapolis : Graphic Universe, [2016] I Series: Cici: a fairy's tale;
    2 I Summary: "Cici, a young fairy, is only joking when she uses her powers
    to play a trick on the popular girl at school. But the changes Cici made to
    her classmate will last forever if she doesn't learn to see the best in people"—
    Provided by publisher.
Identifiers: LCCN 2015036132 I ISBN 9781467761536 (lb : alk. paper) I
    ISBN 9781512411560 (pb : alk. paper) I ISBN 9781512409048 (eb pdf)
Subjects: LCSH: Graphic novels. I CYAC: Graphic novels. I Fairies—Fiction.
    I Magic—Fiction. I Schools—Fiction. I Friendship—Fiction. I Hispanic
    Americans—Fiction.
Classification: LCC PZ7.7.D634 Tr 2016 I DDC 741.5/973—dc23

LC record available at https://lccn.loc.gov/2015036132

Manufactured in the United States of America
2-42975-18116-9/8/2016

For J.B.

—Cori

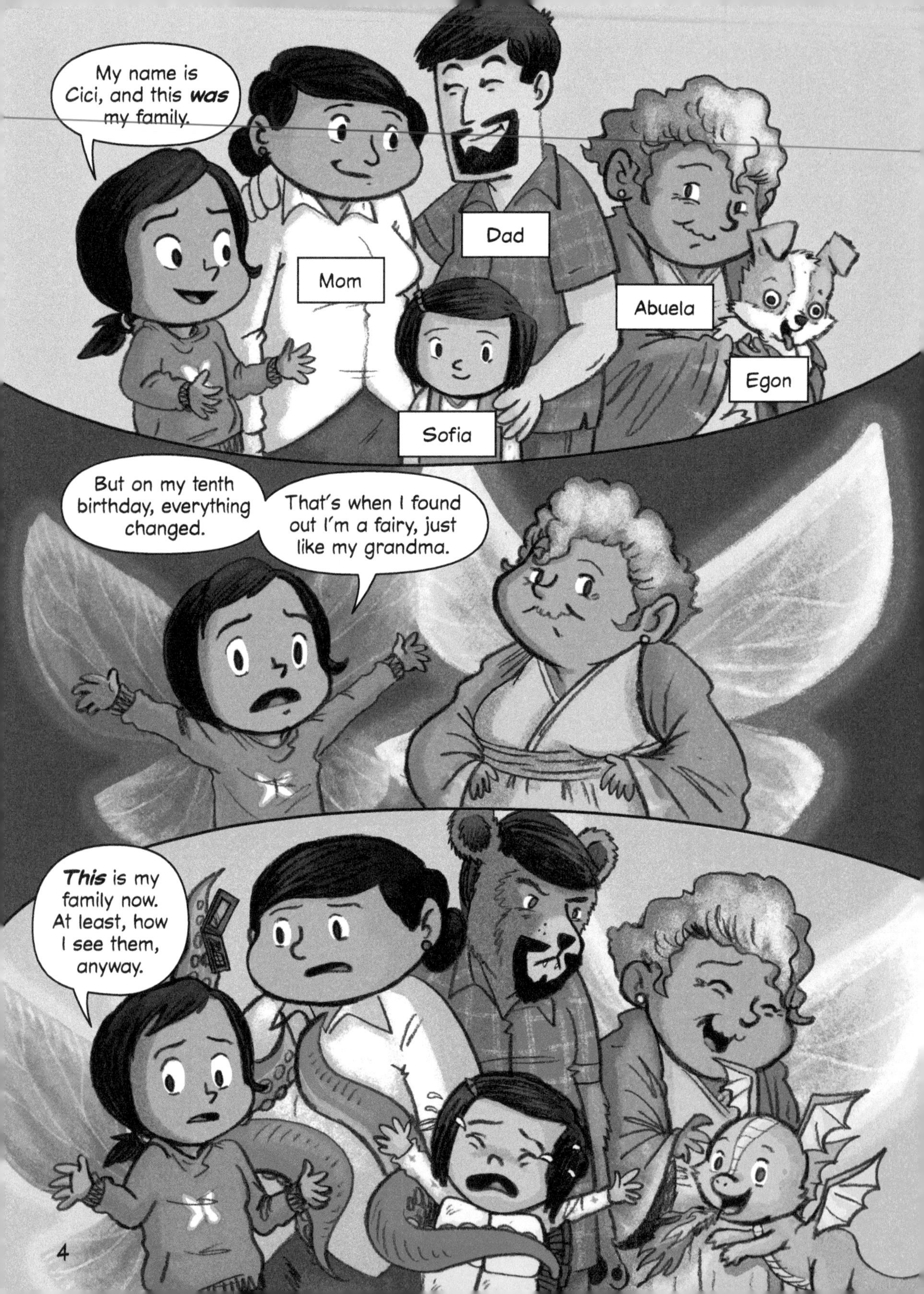
My name is Cici, and this ***was*** my family.
Mom
Dad
Sofia
Abuela
Egon
But on my tenth birthday, everything changed.
That's when I found out I'm a fairy, just like my grandma.
This is my family now. At least, how I see them, anyway.

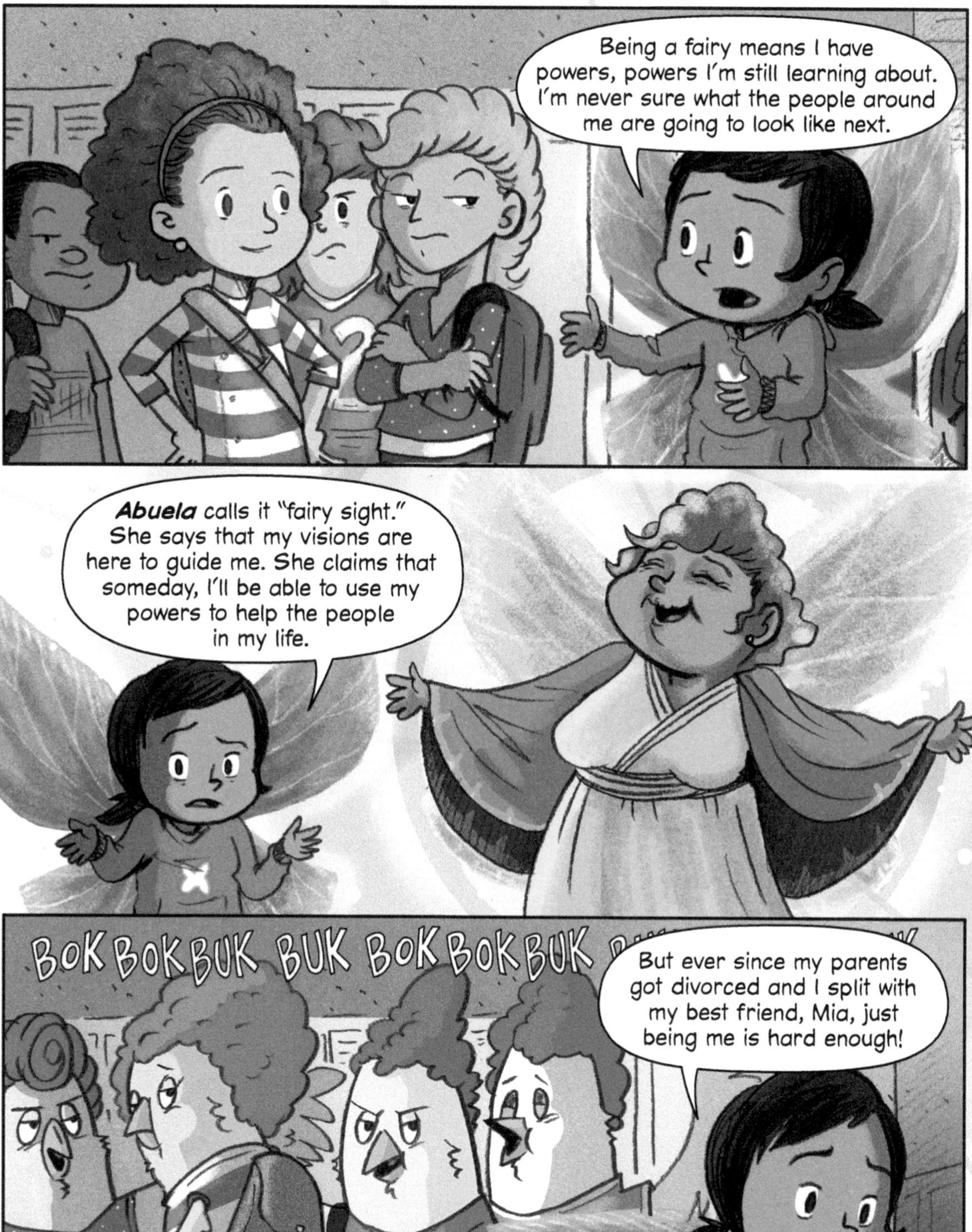
Being a fairy means I have powers, powers I'm still learning about. I'm never sure what the people around me are going to look like next.
Abuela calls it "fairy sight." She says that my visions are here to guide me. She claims that someday, I'll be able to use my powers to help the people in my life.
BOK BOK BUK BUK BOK BOK BUK
But ever since my parents got divorced and I split with my best friend, Mia, just being me is hard enough!

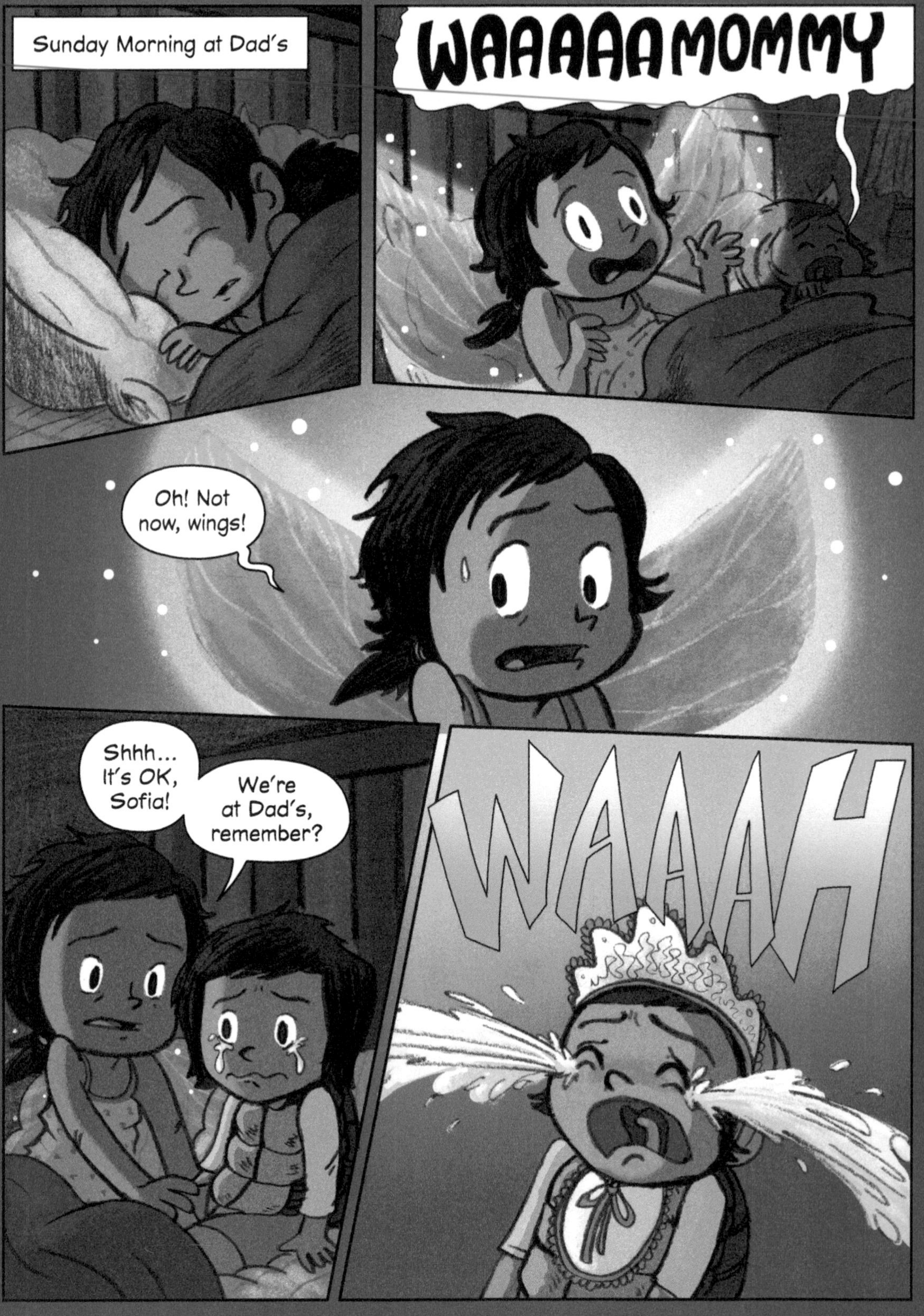
Sunday Morning at Dad's
WAAAAAMOMMY
Oh! Not now, wings!
Shhh... It's OK, Sofia!
We're at Dad's, remember?
WAAAH

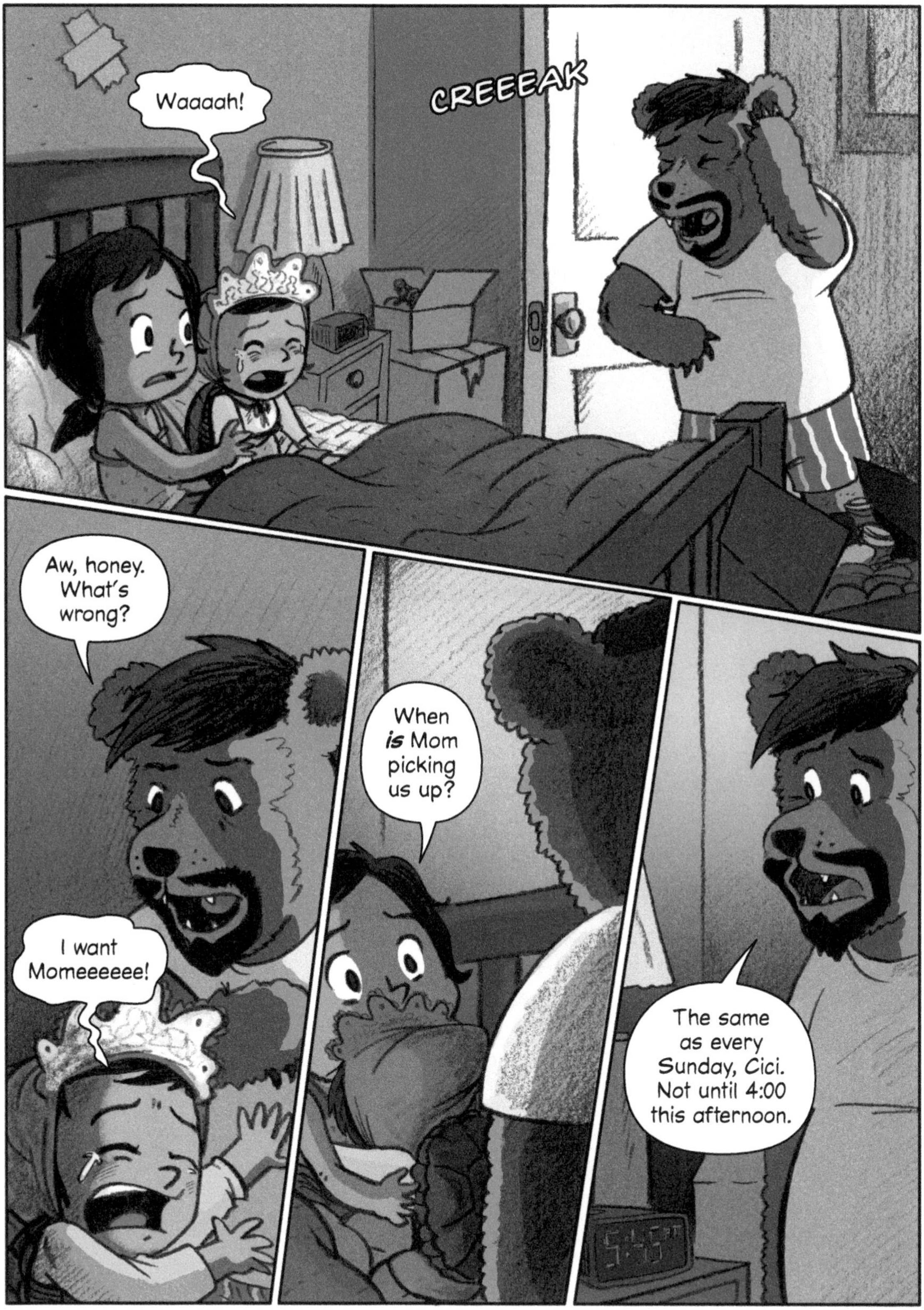
Waaaah!
CREEEAK
Aw, honey. What's wrong?
I want Momeeeeee!
When *is* Mom picking us up?
The same as every Sunday, Cici. Not until 4:00 this afternoon.

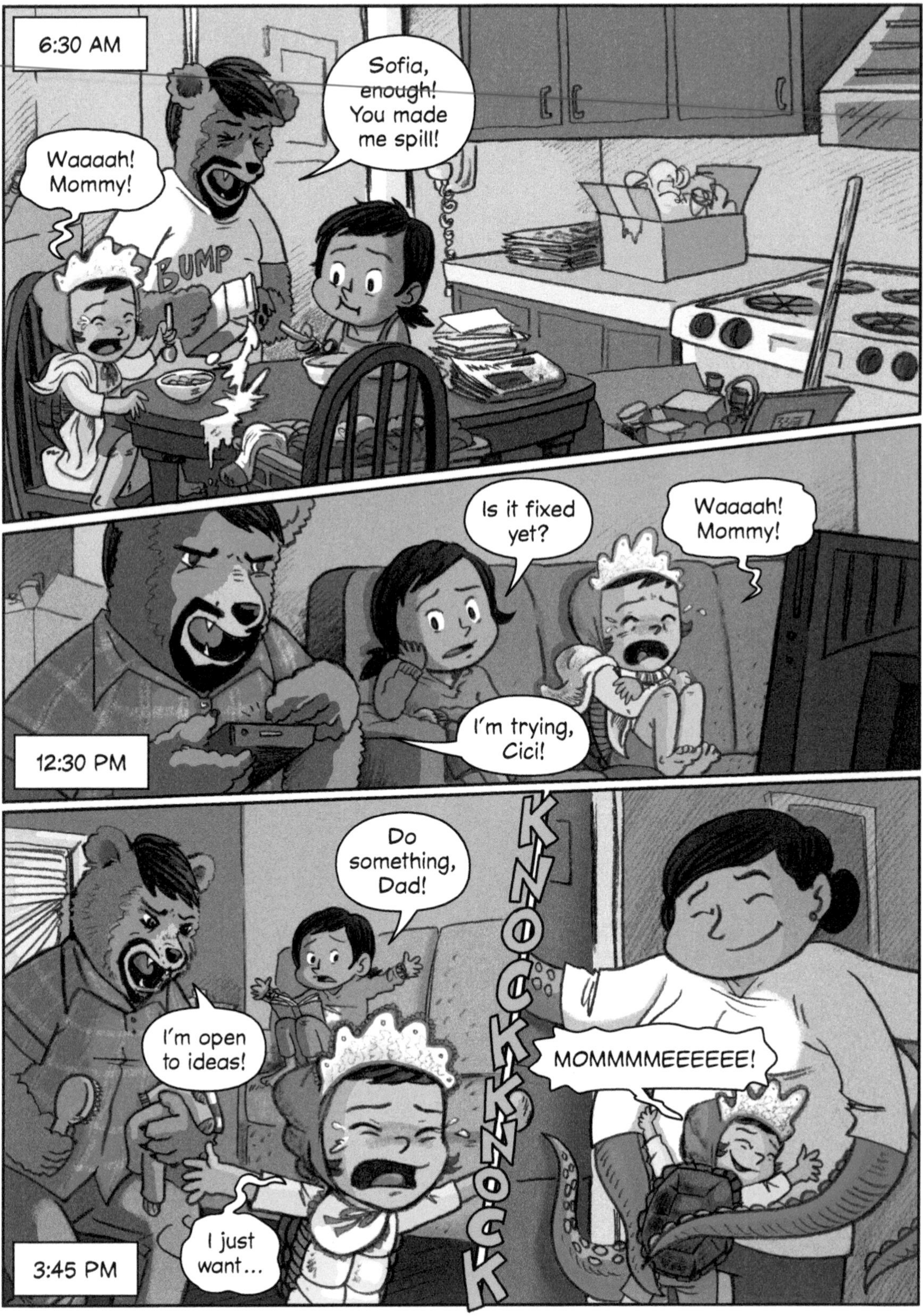
6:30 AM
Waaaah! Mommy!
Sofia, enough! You made me spill!
BUMP
Is it fixed yet?
Waaaah! Mommy!
I'm trying, Cici!
12:30 PM
Do something, Dad!
KNOCK KNOCK KNOCK
I'm open to ideas!
MOMMMMEEEEEE!
I just want...
3:45 PM

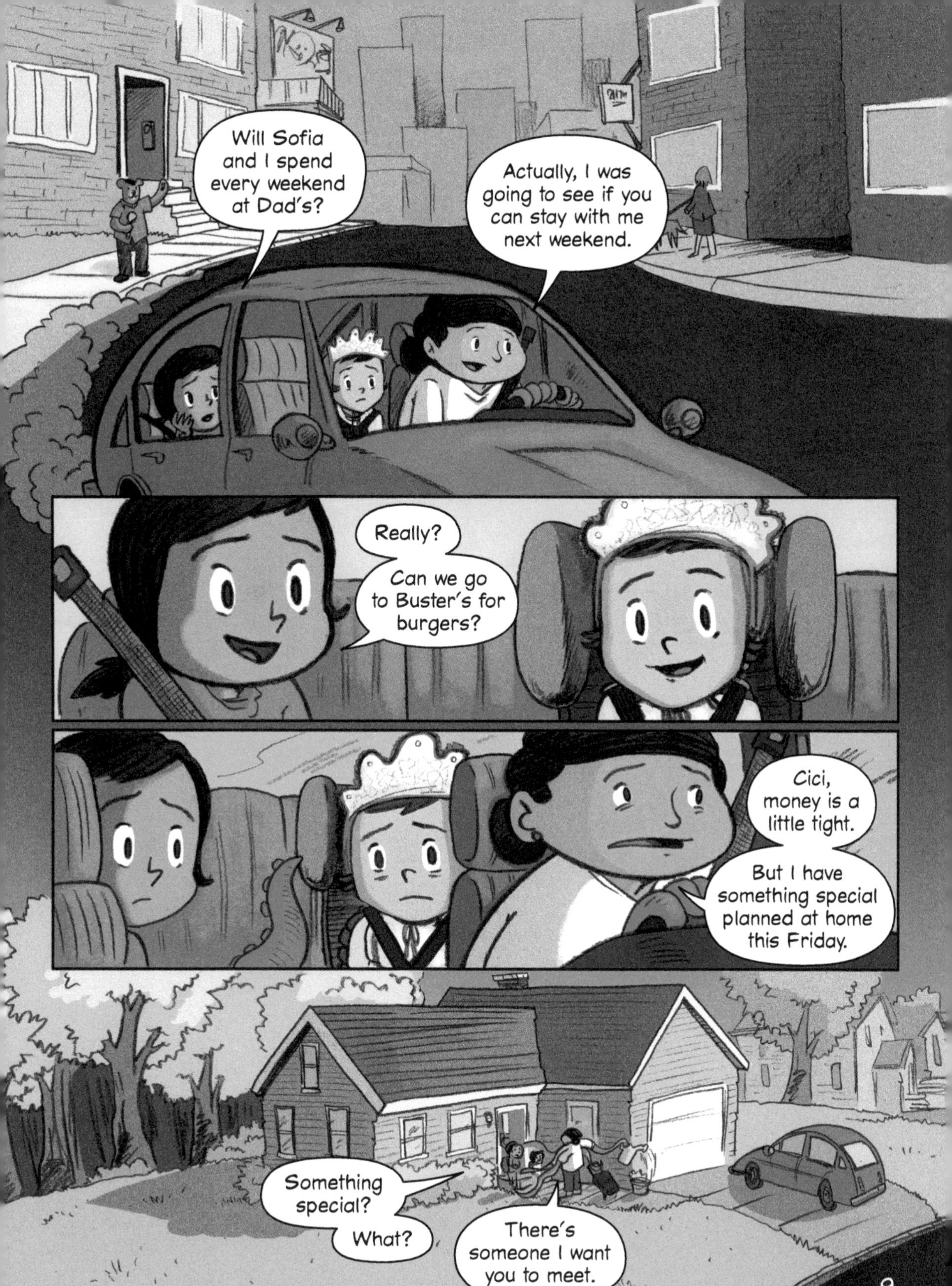
Will Sofia and I spend every weekend at Dad's?
Actually, I was going to see if you can stay with me next weekend.
Really?
Can we go to Buster's for burgers?
Cici, money is a little tight.
But I have something special planned at home this Friday.
Something special?
What?
There's someone I want you to meet.

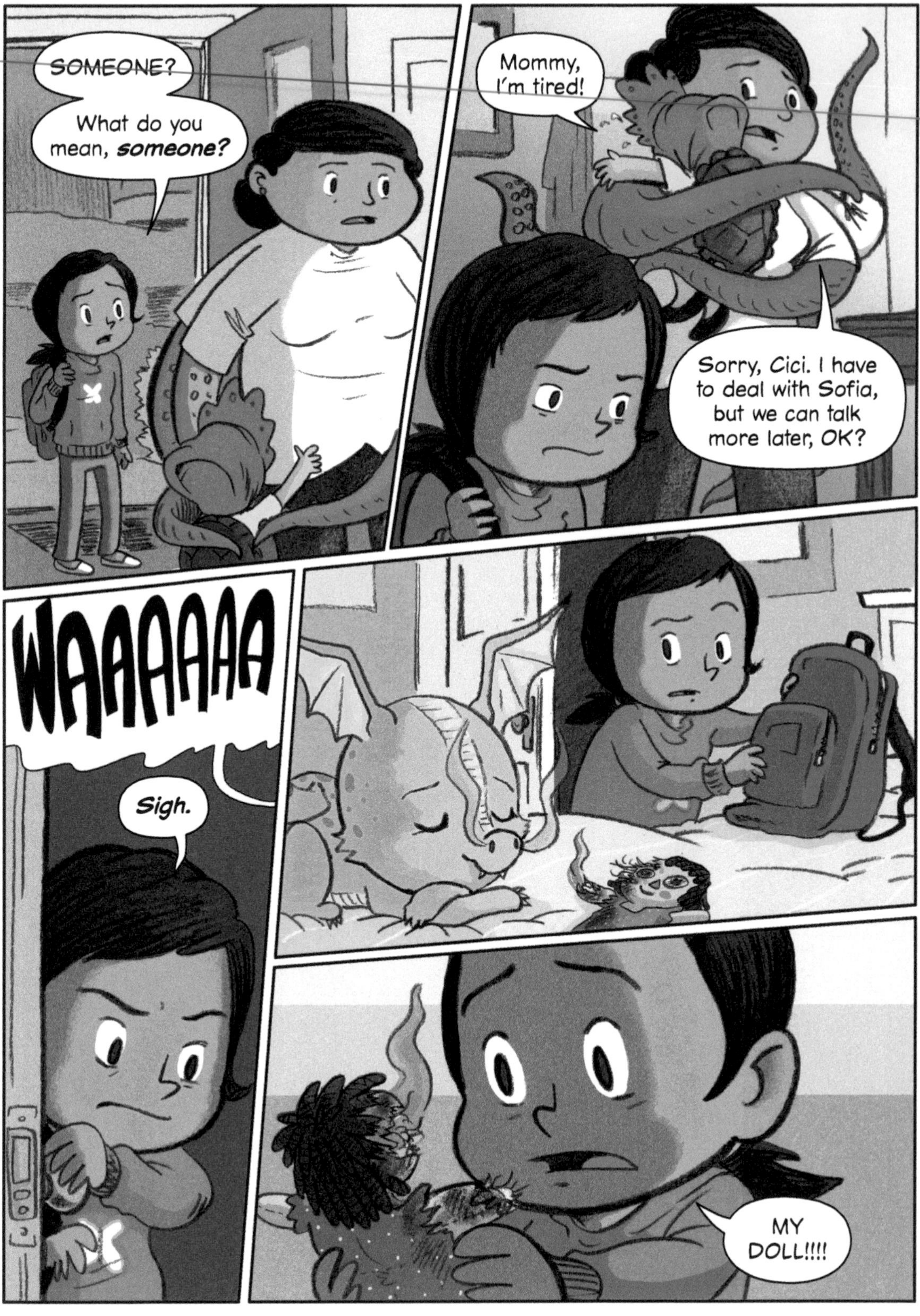
SOMEONE?
What do you mean, someone?
Mommy, I'm tired!
Sorry, Cici. I have to deal with Sofia, but we can talk more later, OK?
WAAAAAA
Sigh.
MY DOLL!!!!

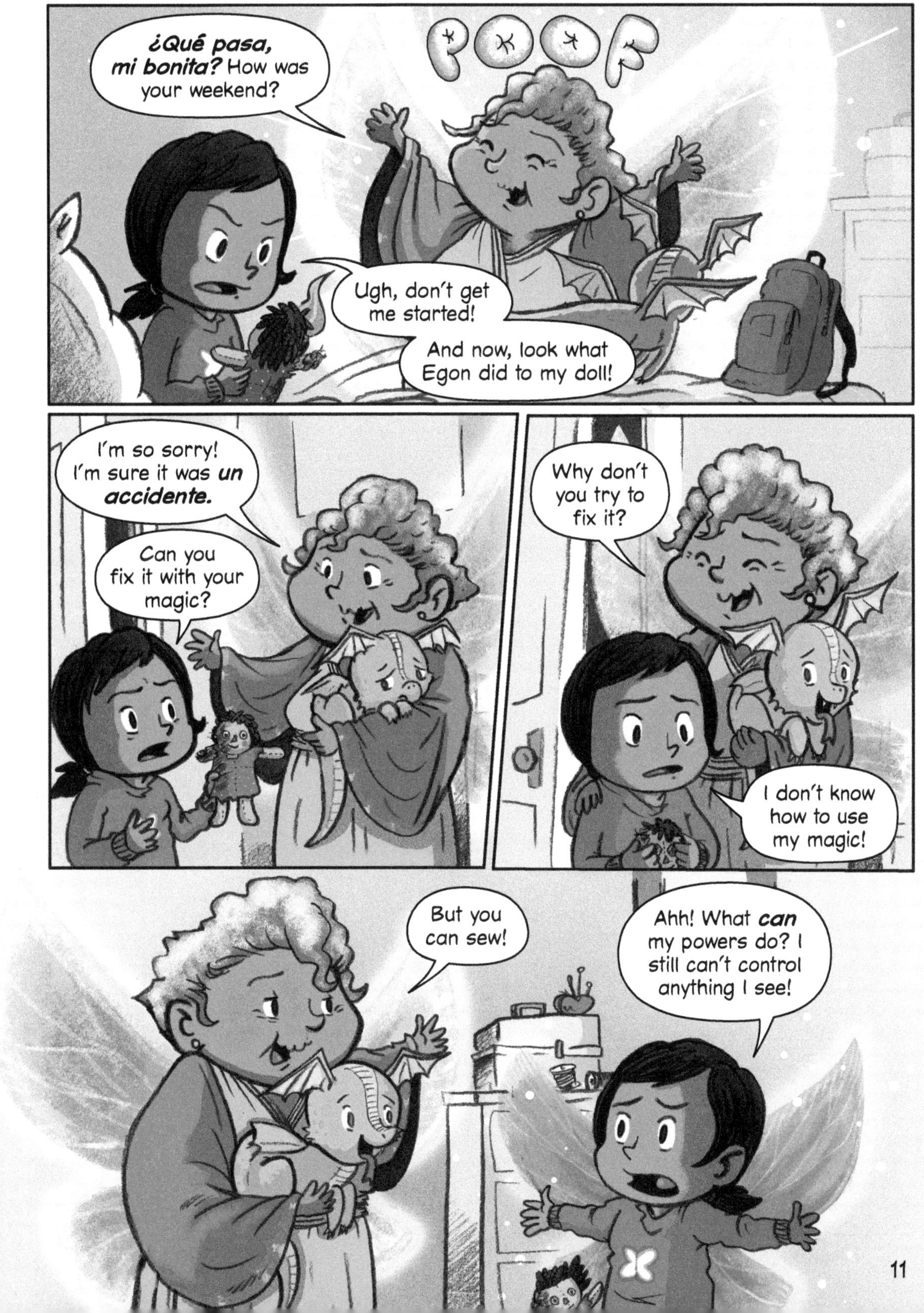
POOF
¿Qué pasa, mi bonita? How was your weekend?
Ugh, don't get me started!
And now, look what Egon did to my doll!
I'm so sorry! I'm sure it was ***un accidente.***
Can you fix it with your magic?
Why don't you try to fix it?
I don't know how to use my magic!
But you can sew!
Ahh! What ***can*** my powers do? I still can't control anything I see!

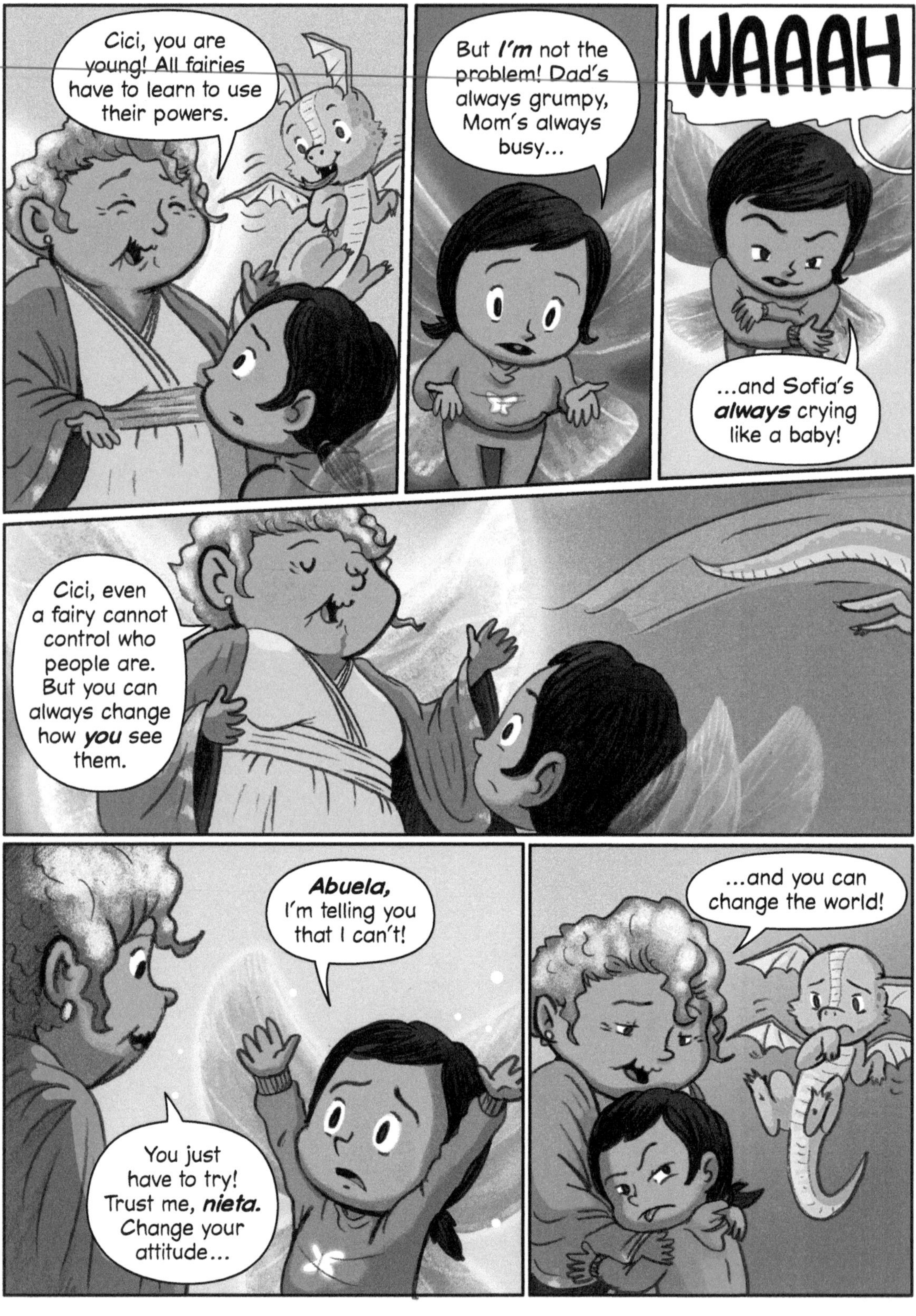

Cici, you are young! All fairies have to learn to use their powers.
But *I'm* not the problem! Dad's always grumpy, Mom's always busy...
WAAAH
...and Sofia's ***always*** crying like a baby!
Cici, even a fairy cannot control who people are. But you can always change how ***you*** see them.
Abuela, I'm telling you that I can't!
You just have to try! Trust me, ***nieta.*** Change your attitude...
...and you can change the world!

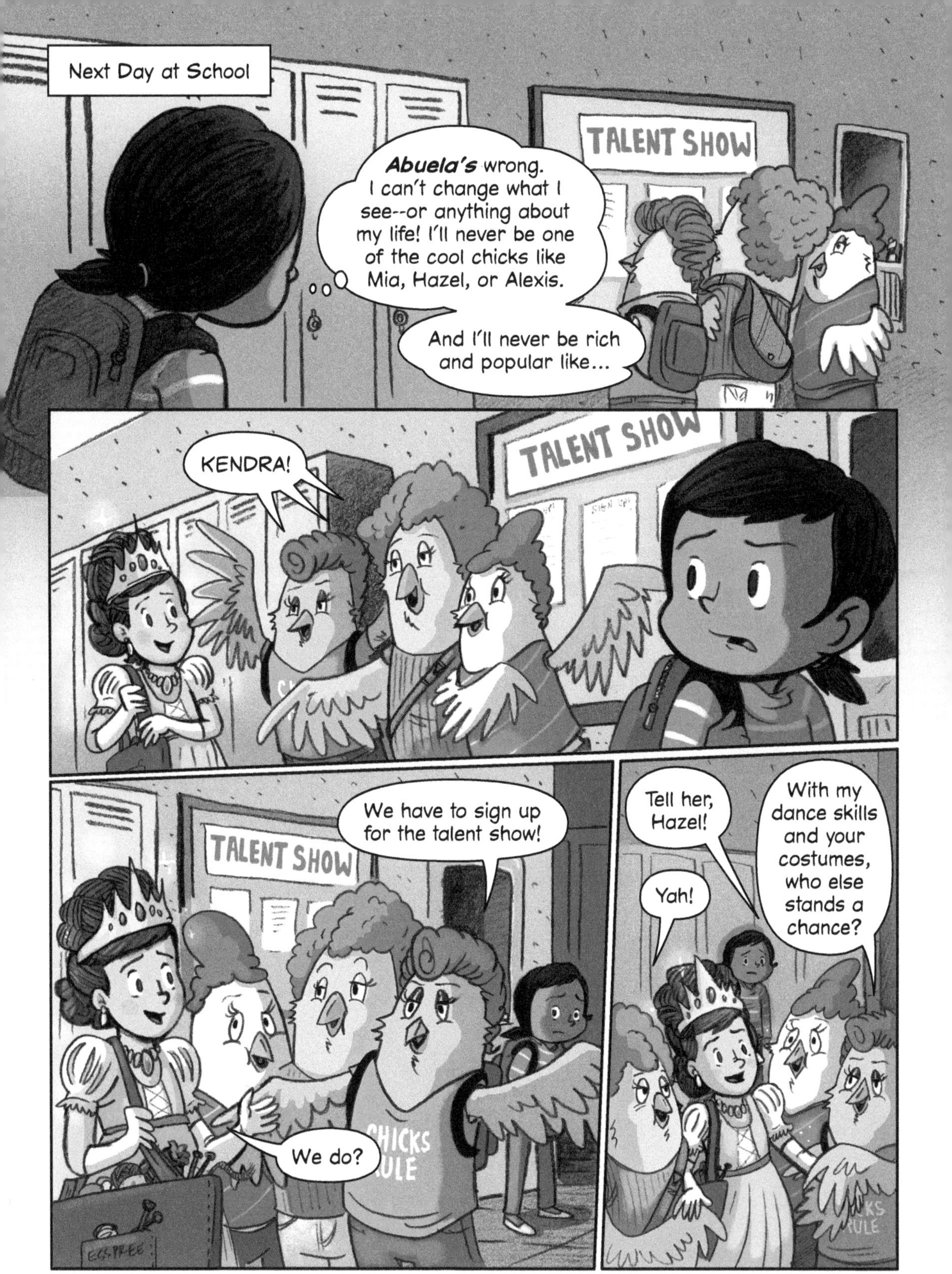
Next Day at School
TALENT SHOW
Abuela's wrong. I can't change what I see--or anything about my life! I'll never be one of the cool chicks like Mia, Hazel, or Alexis.
And I'll never be rich and popular like...
TALENT SHOW
KENDRA!
TALENT SHOW
We have to sign up for the talent show!
We do?
CHICKS RULE
Tell her, Hazel!
Yah!
With my dance skills and your costumes, who else stands a chance?

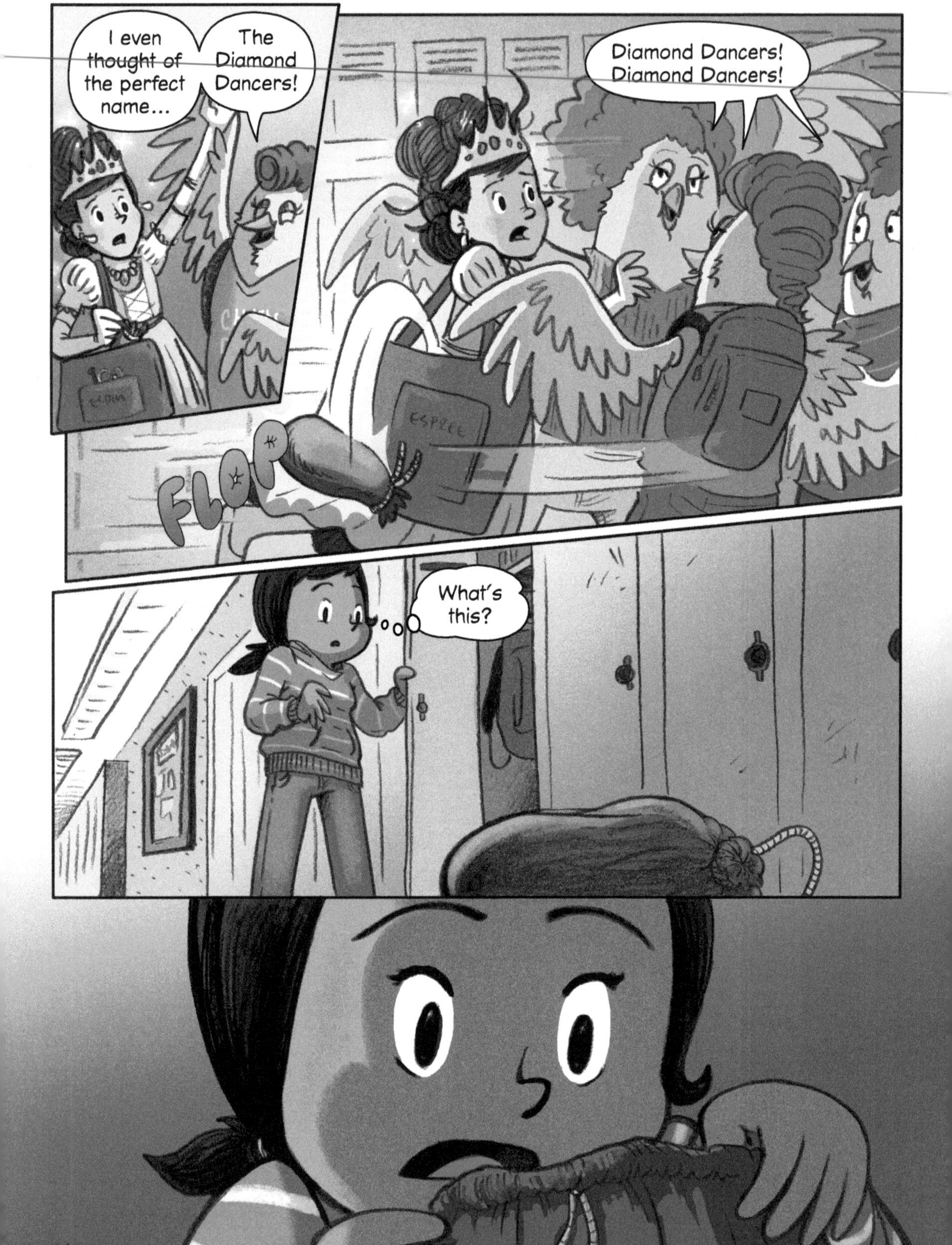

I even thought of the perfect name...
The Diamond Dancers!
Diamond Dancers! Diamond Dancers!
FLOP
What's this?

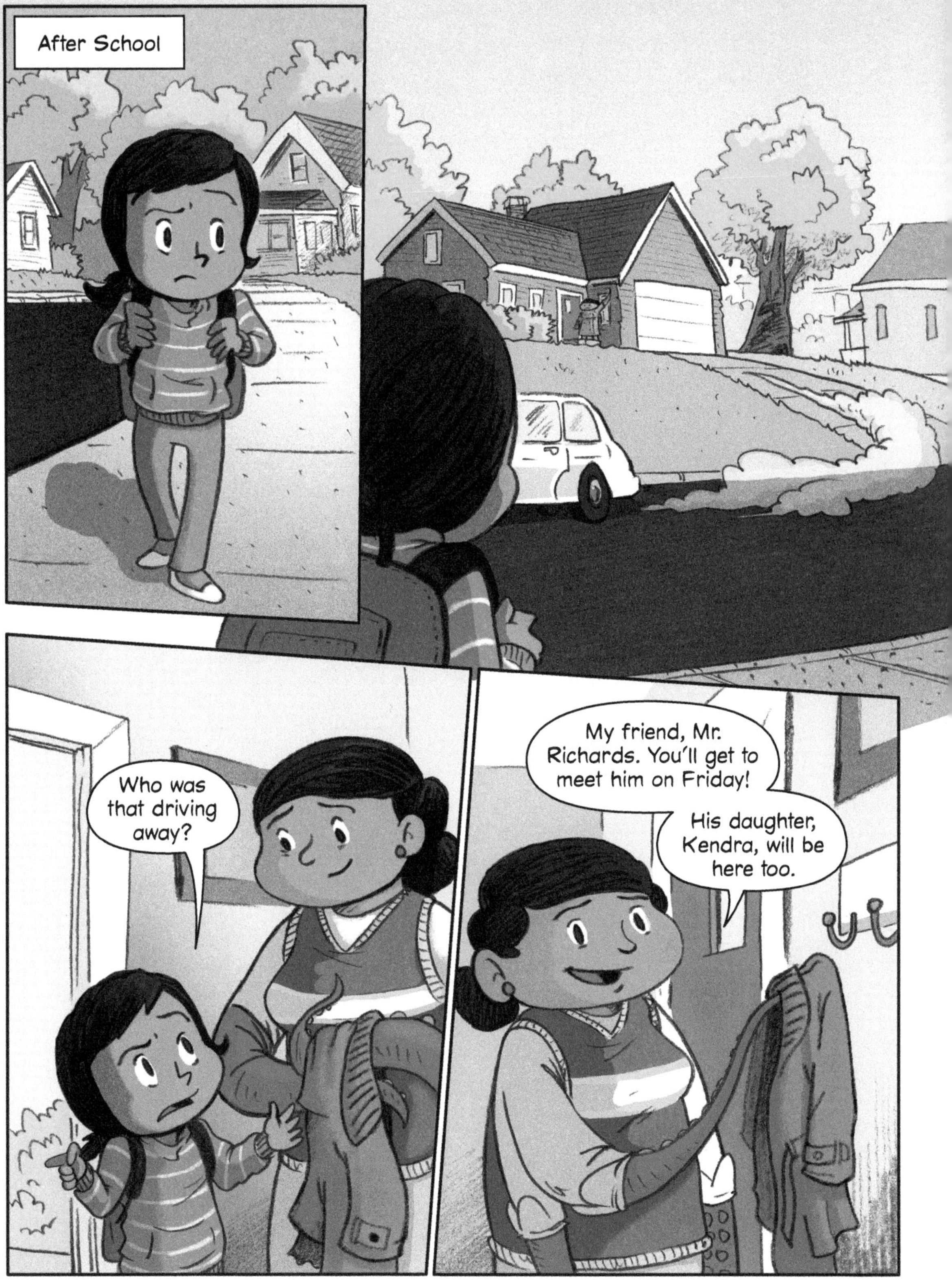
After School
Who was that driving away?
My friend, Mr. Richards. You'll get to meet him on Friday!
His daughter, Kendra, will be here too.

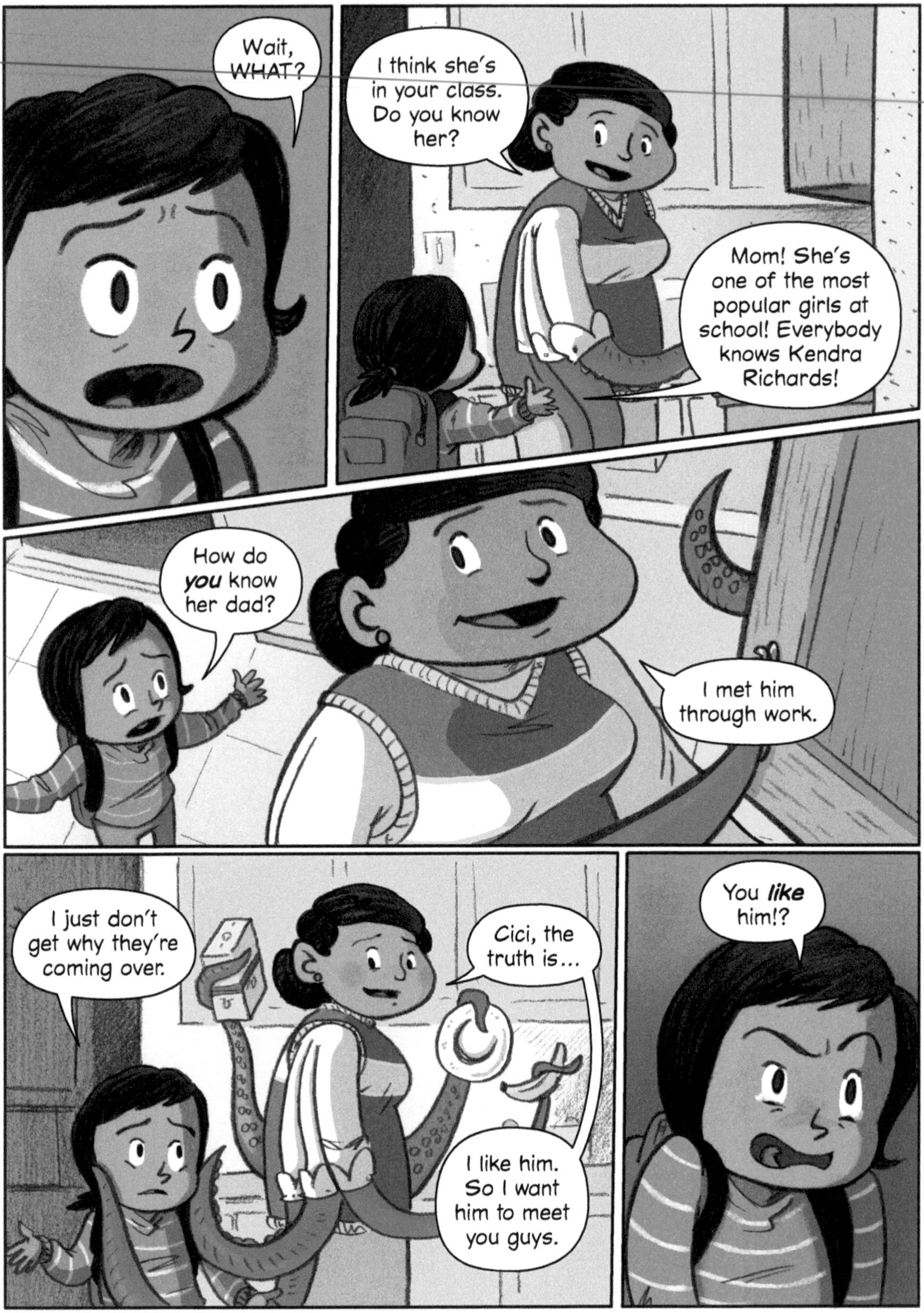
Wait, WHAT?
I think she's in your class. Do you know her?
Mom! She's one of the most popular girls at school! Everybody knows Kendra Richards!
How do *you* know her dad?
I met him through work.
I just don't get why they're coming over.
Cici, the truth is...
I like him. So I want him to meet you guys.
You *like* him!?

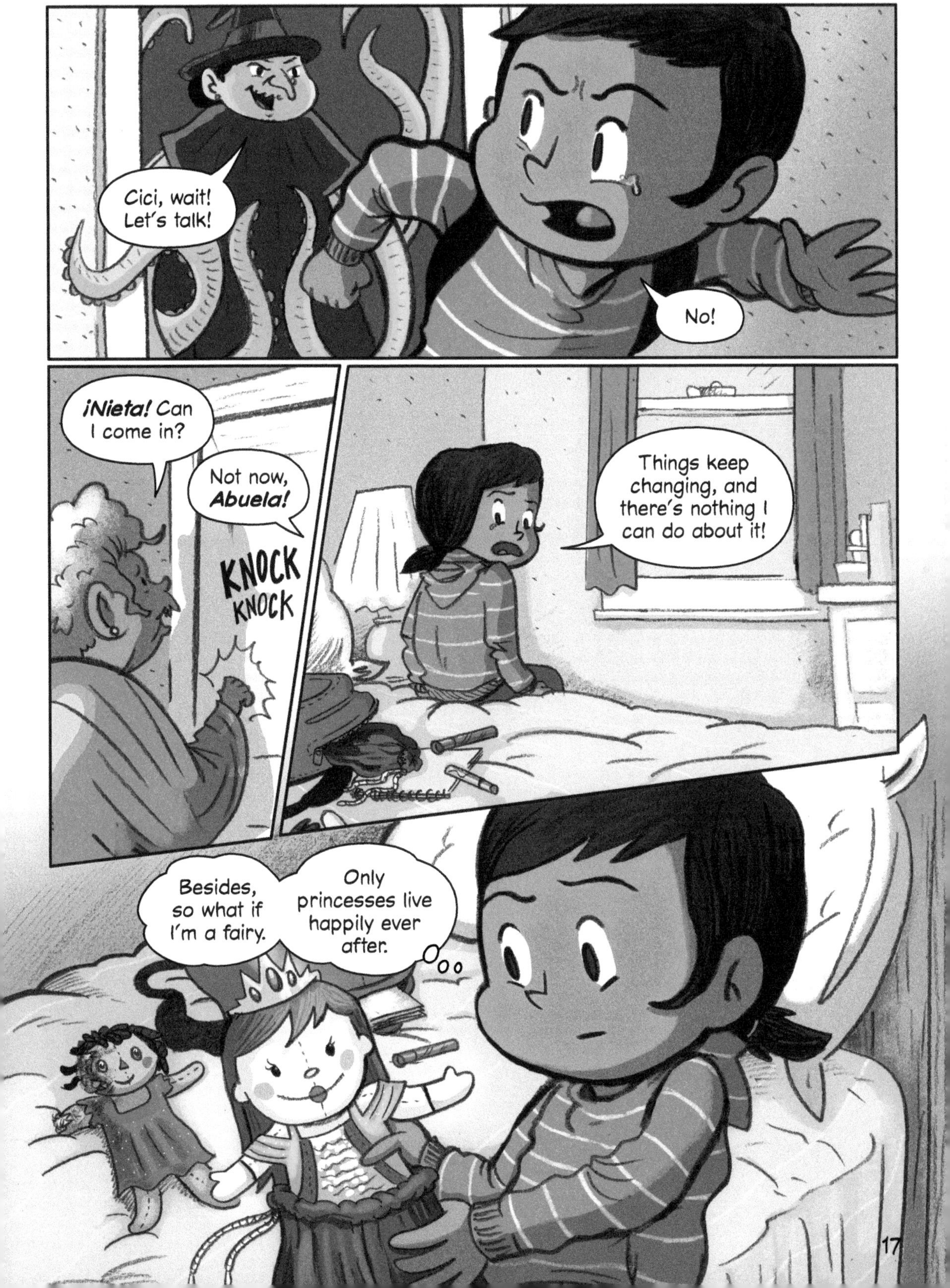

Cici, wait!
Let's talk!
No!
¡Nieta! Can I come in?
Not now, Abuela!
KNOCK KNOCK
Things keep changing, and there's nothing I can do about it!
Besides, so what if I'm a fairy.
Only princesses live happily ever after.

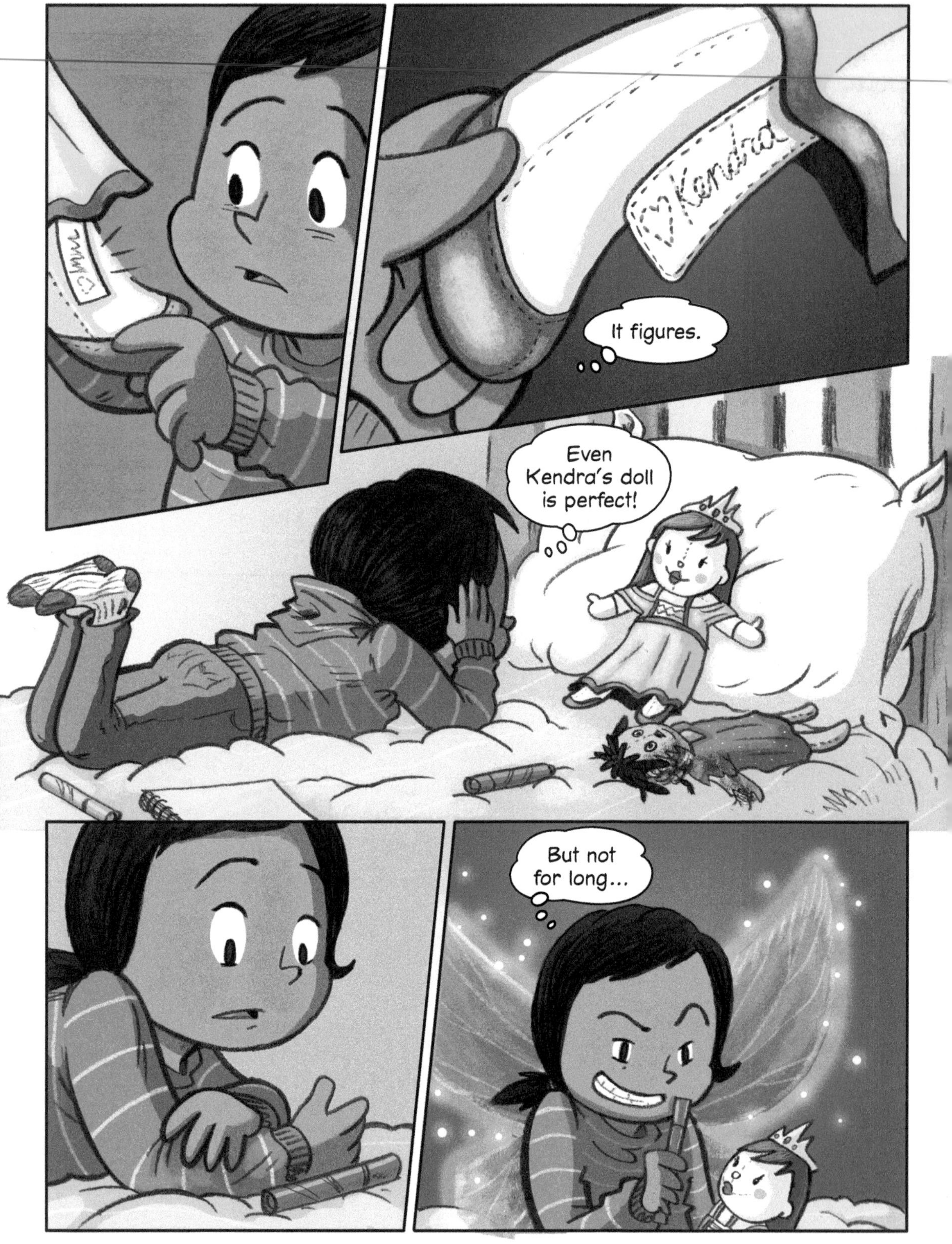

Kendra
It figures.
Even Kendra's doll is perfect!
But not for long...

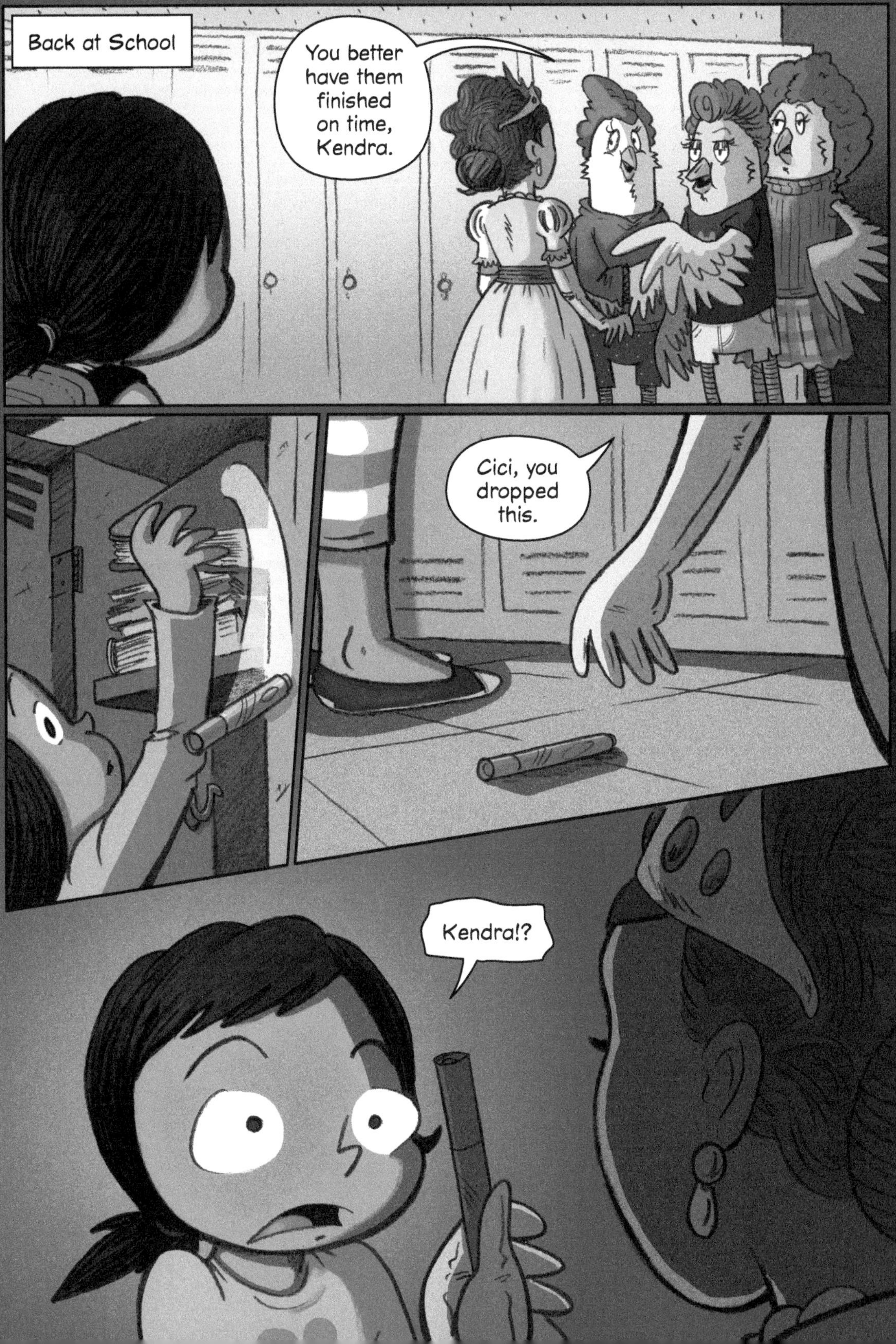
Back at School
You better have them finished on time, Kendra.
Cici, you dropped this.
Kendra!?

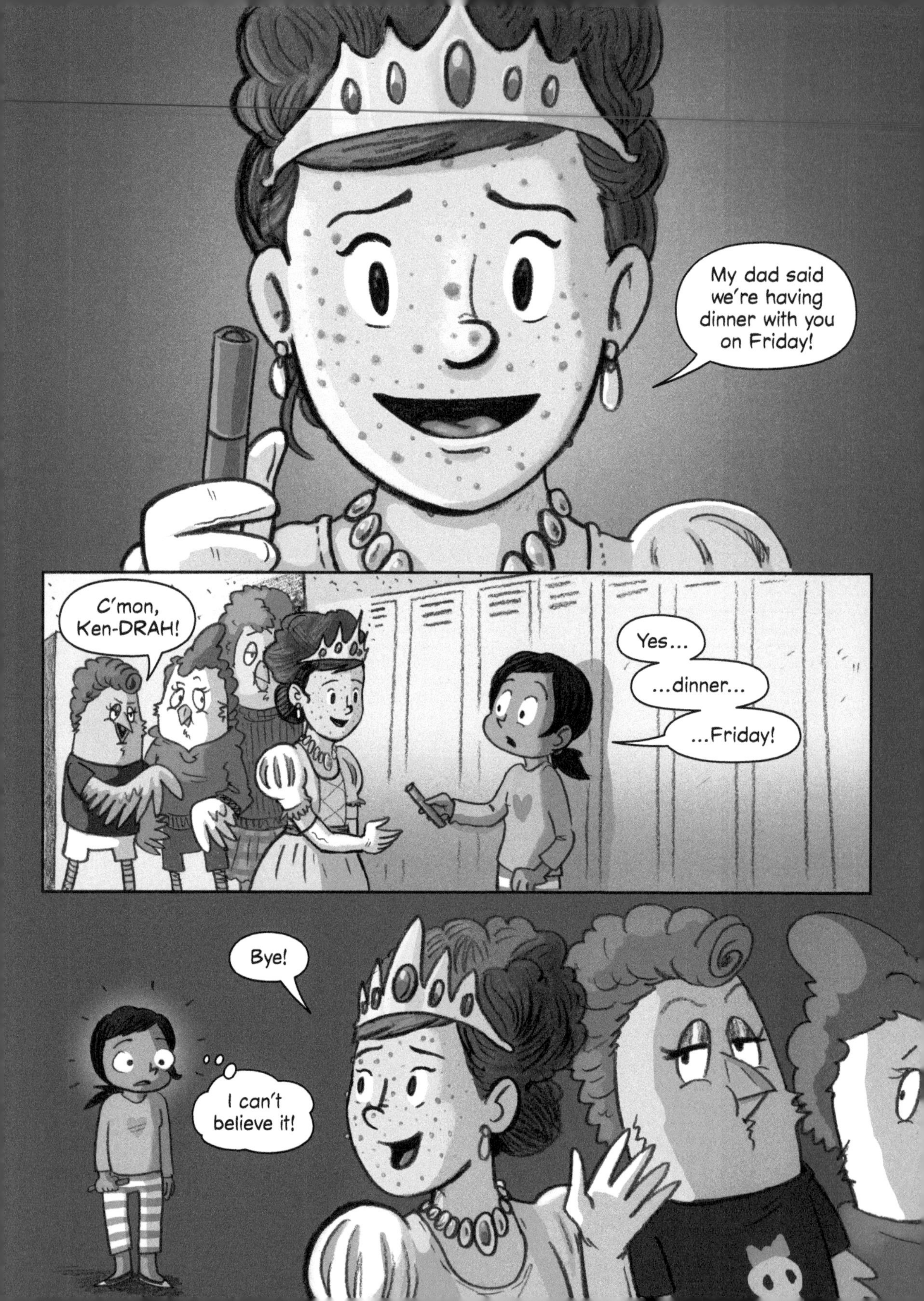
My dad said we're having dinner with you on Friday!
C'mon, Ken-DRAH!
Yes...
...dinner...
...Friday!
Bye!
I can't believe it!

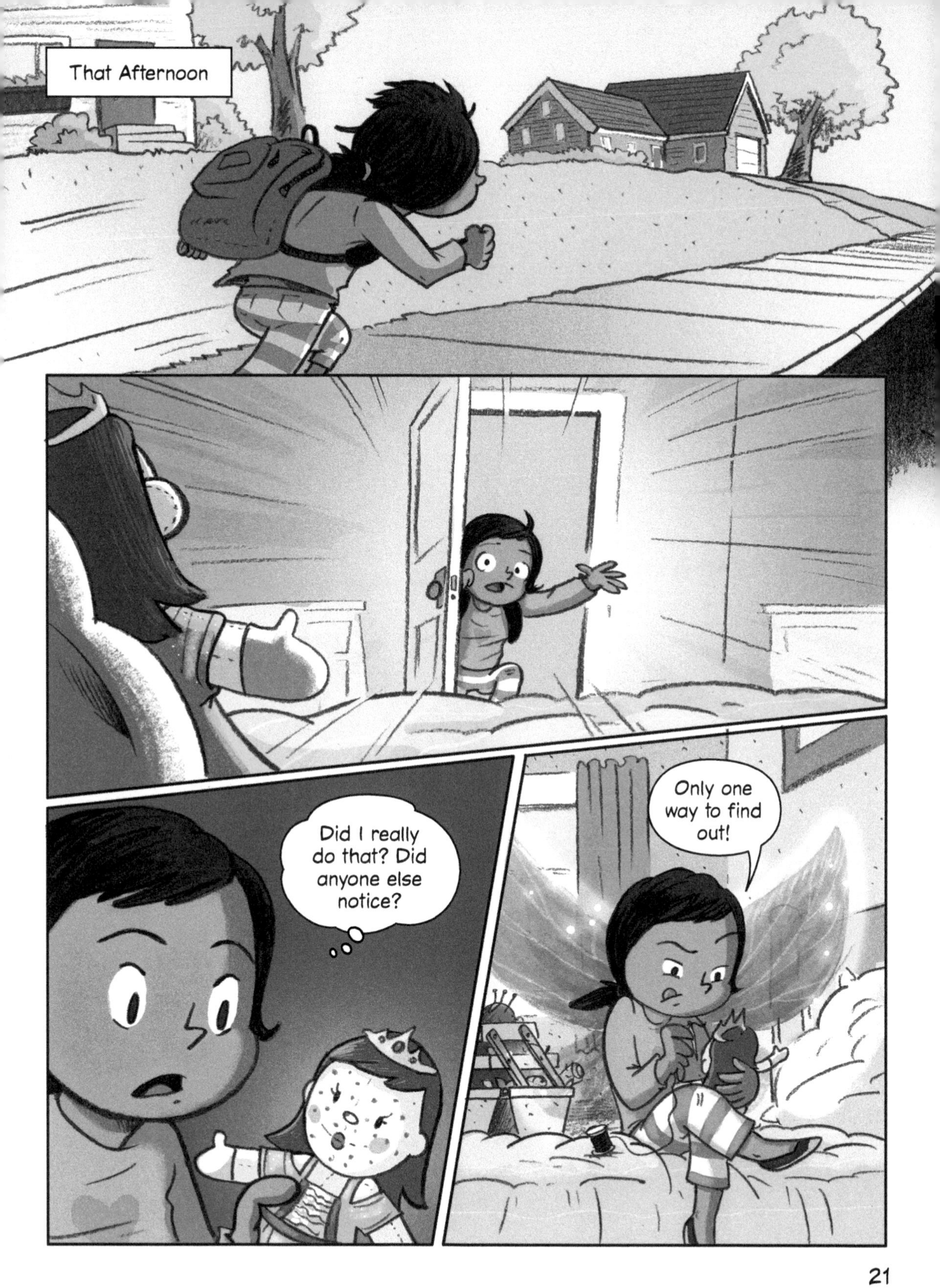
That Afternoon
Did I really do that? Did anyone else notice?
Only one way to find out!

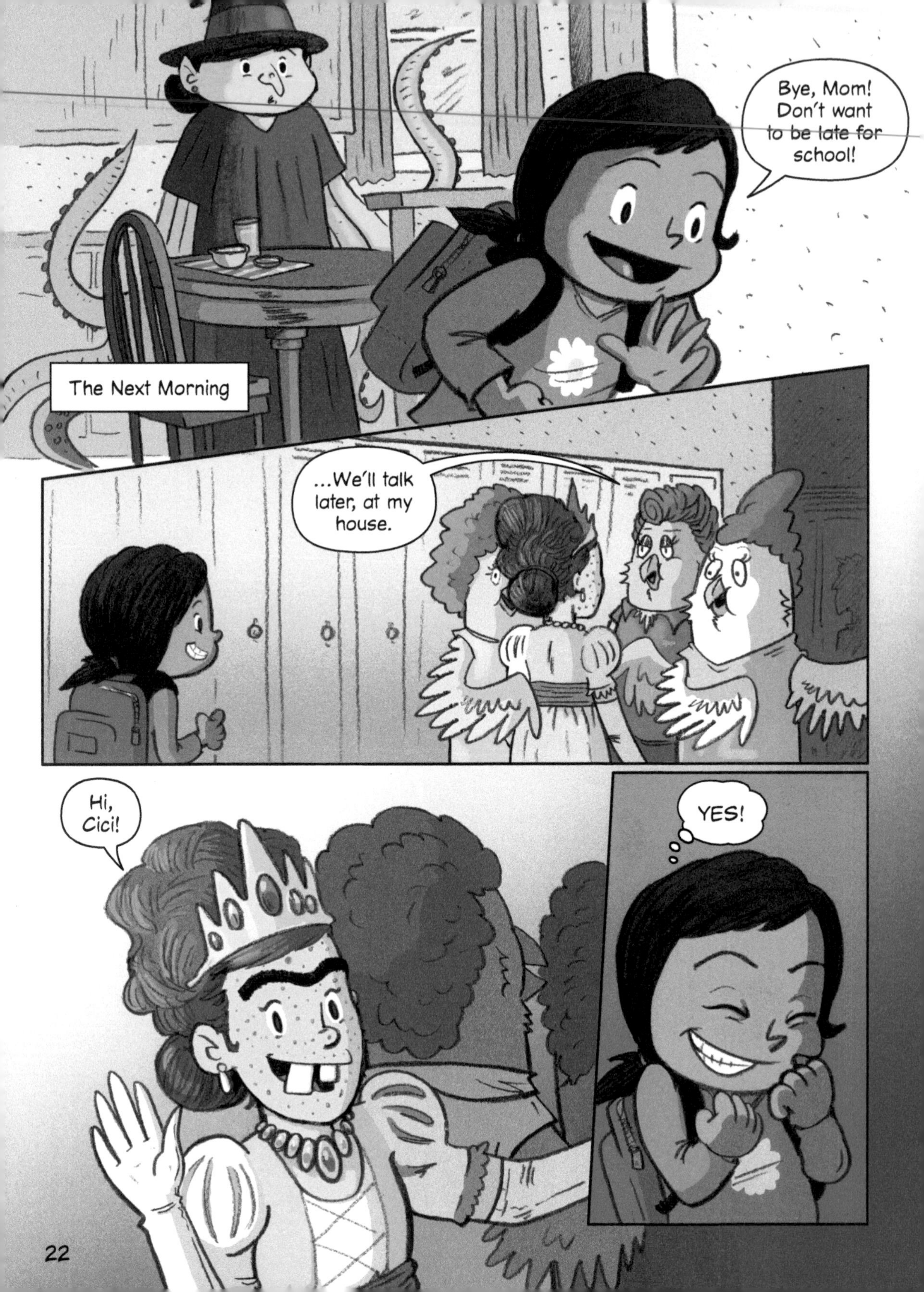
Bye, Mom! Don't want to be late for school!
The Next Morning
...We'll talk later, at my house.
Hi, Cici!
YES!

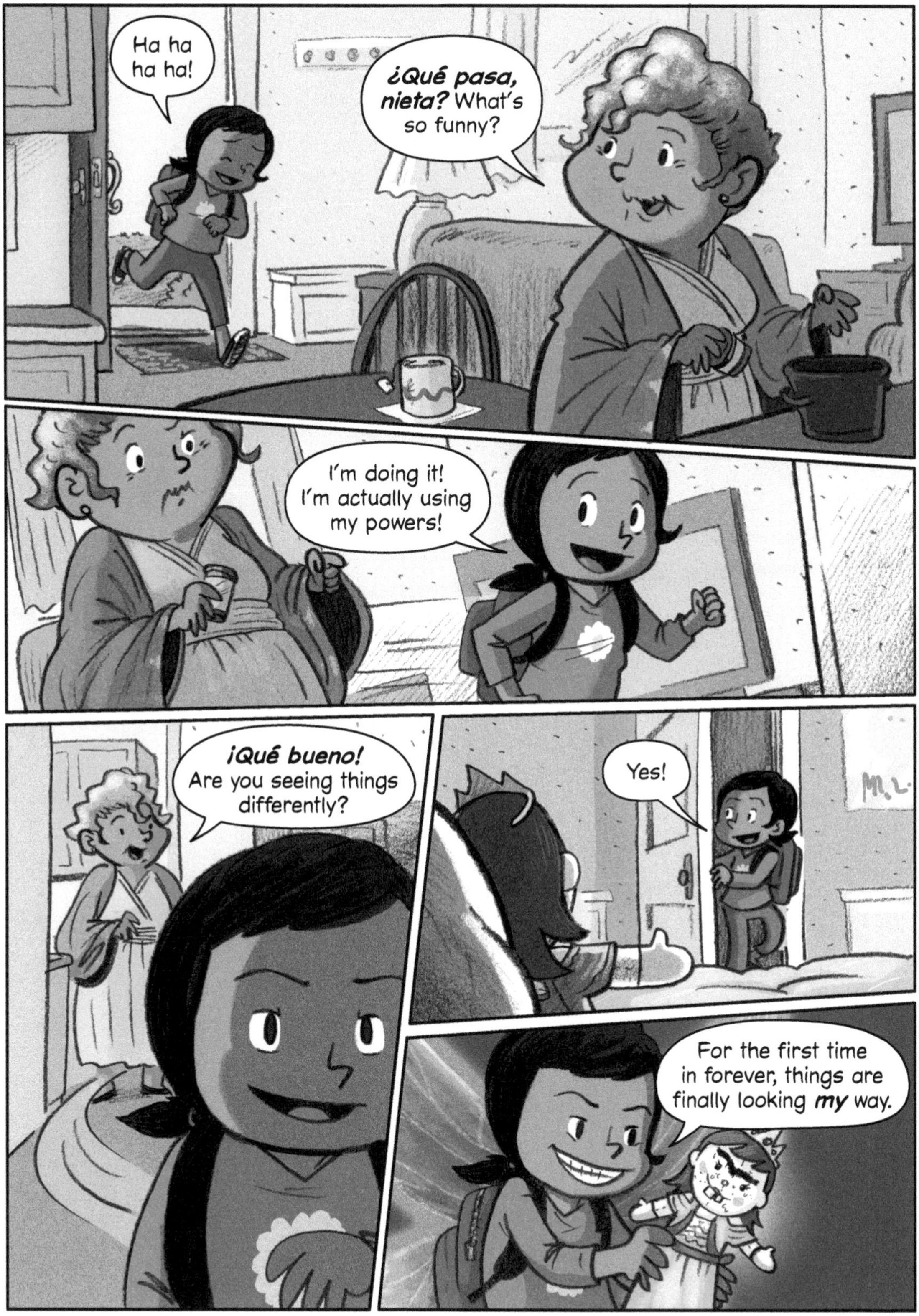
Ha ha ha ha!
¿Qué pasa, nieta? What's so funny?
I'm doing it! I'm actually using my powers!
¡Qué bueno! Are you seeing things differently?
Yes!
For the first time in forever, things are finally looking *my* way.

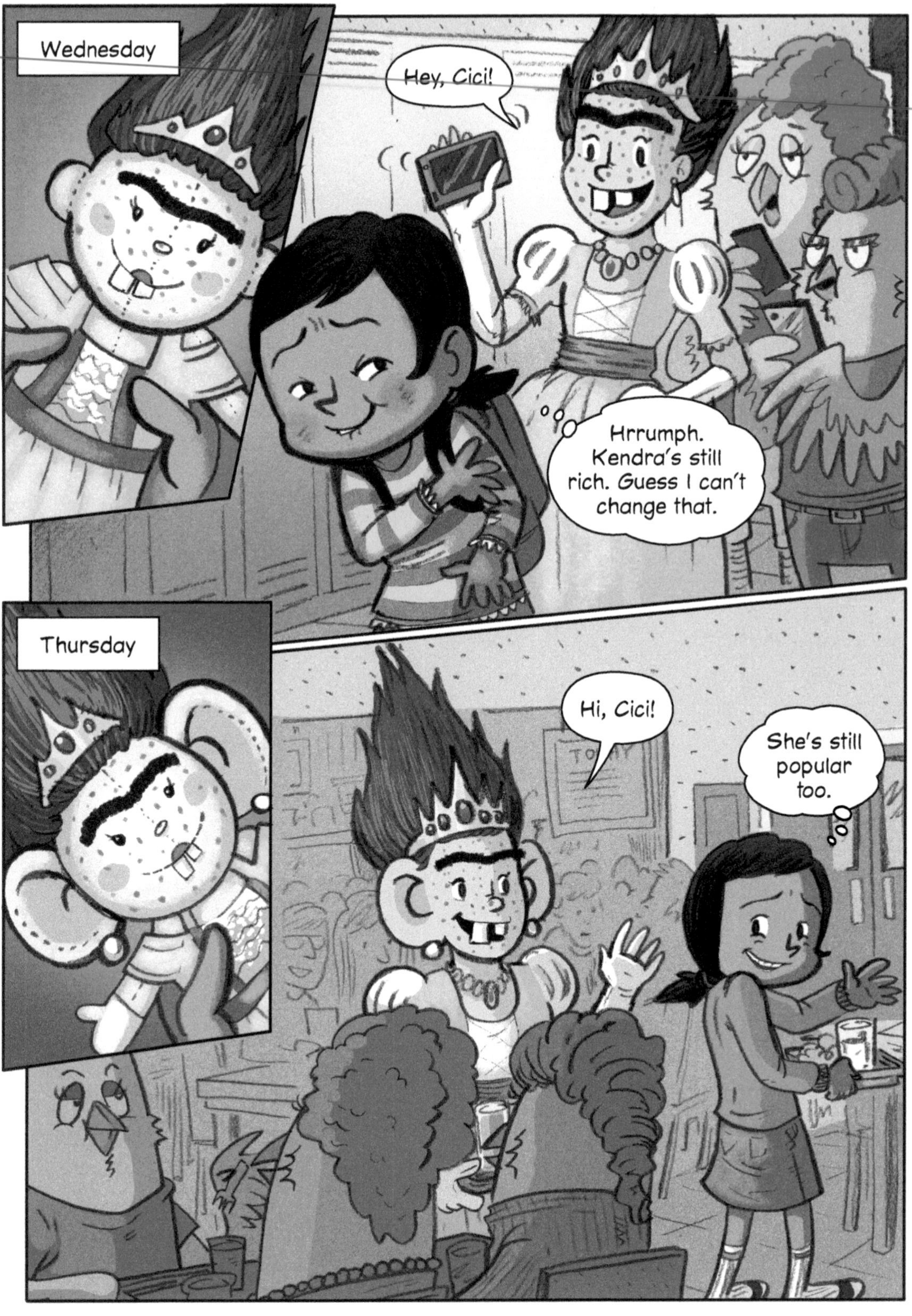
Wednesday
Hey, Cici!
Hrrumph. Kendra's still rich. Guess I can't change that.
Thursday
Hi, Cici!
She's still popular too.

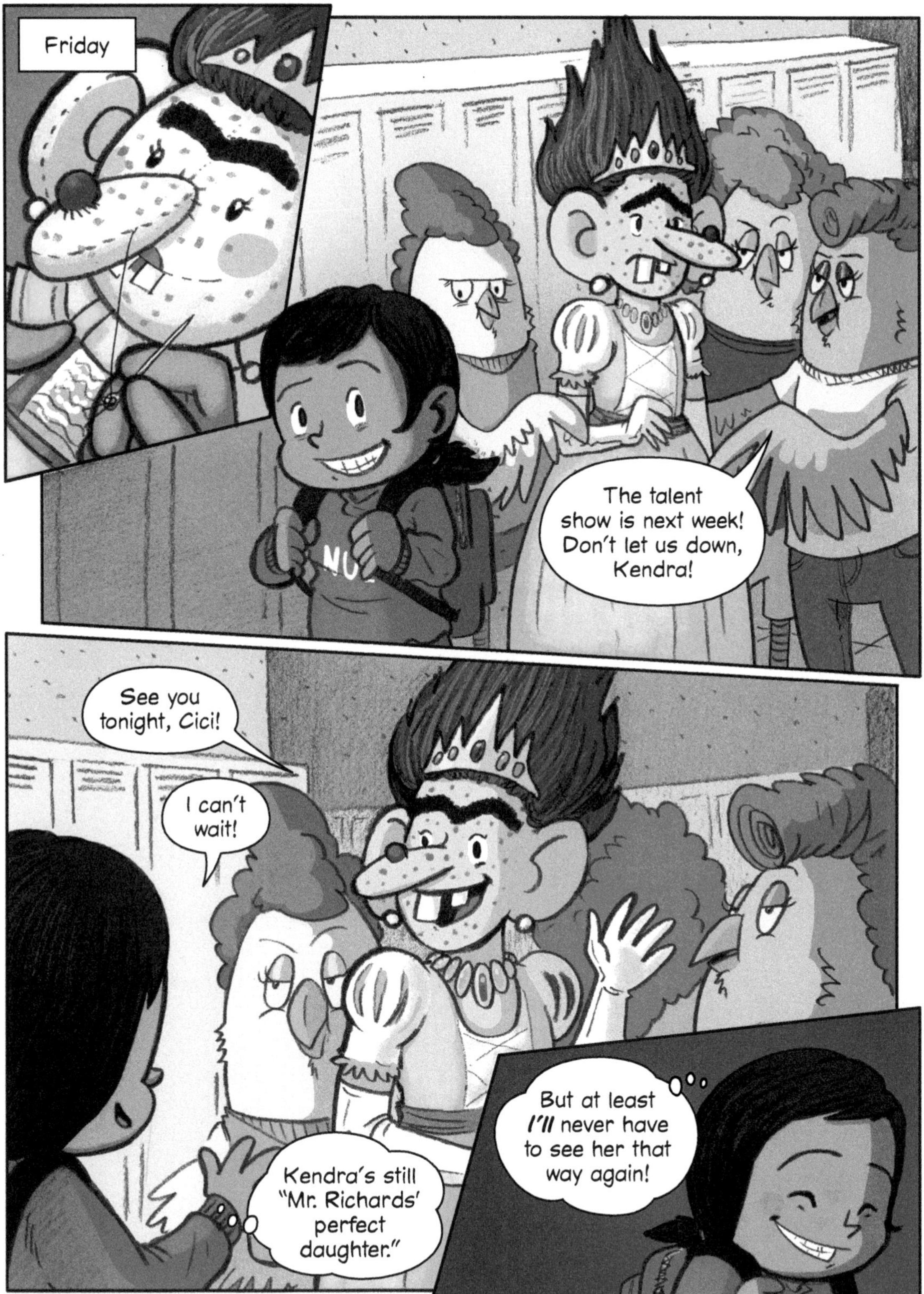
Friday
The talent show is next week! Don't let us down, Kendra!
See you tonight, Cici!
I can't wait!
Kendra's still "Mr. Richards' perfect daughter."
But at least *I'll* never have to see her that way again!

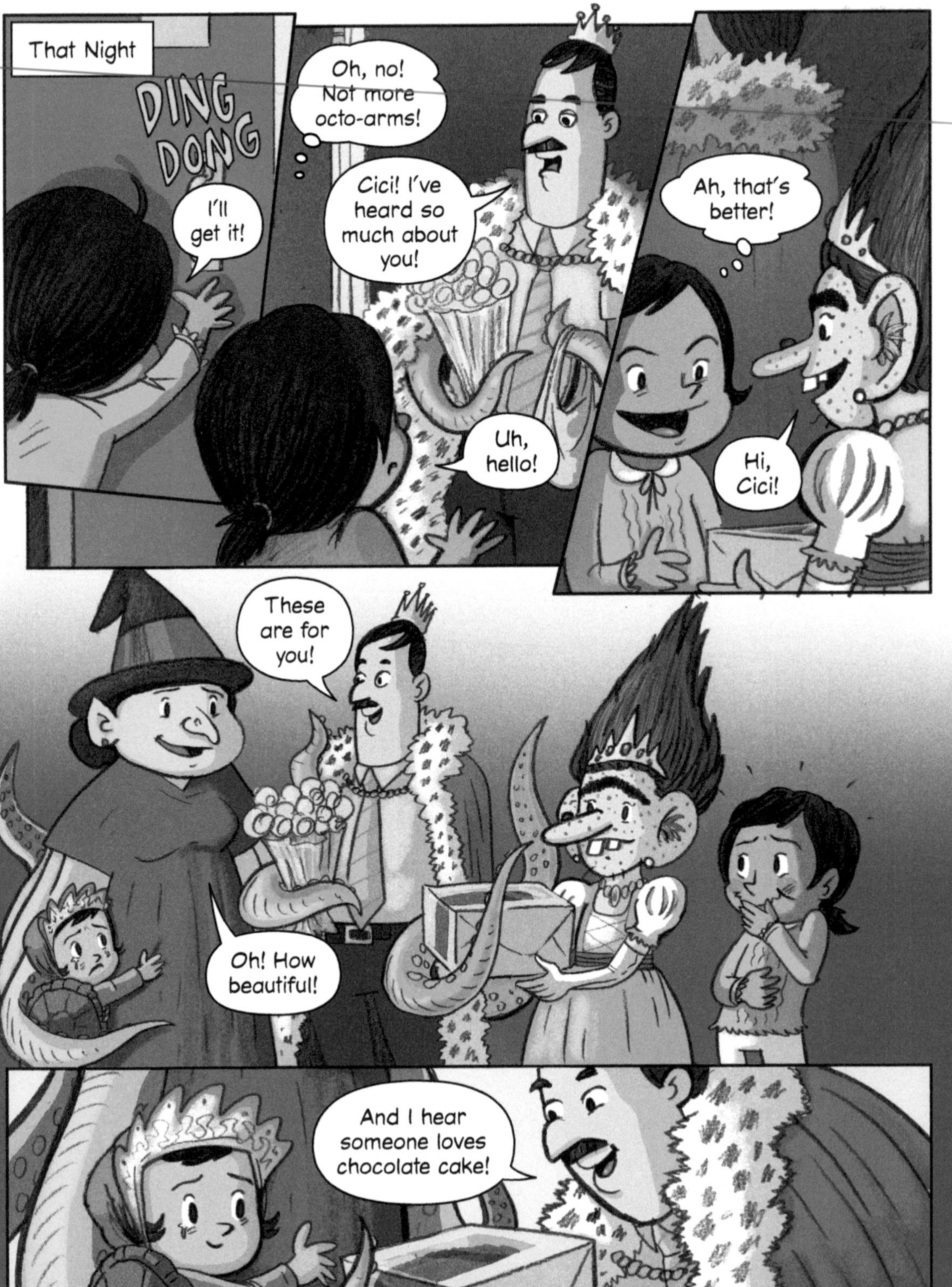
That Night
DING DONG
I'll get it!
Oh, no! Not more octo-arms!
Cici! I've heard so much about you!
Uh, hello!
Ah, that's better!
Hi, Cici!
These are for you!
Oh! How beautiful!
And I hear someone loves chocolate cake!

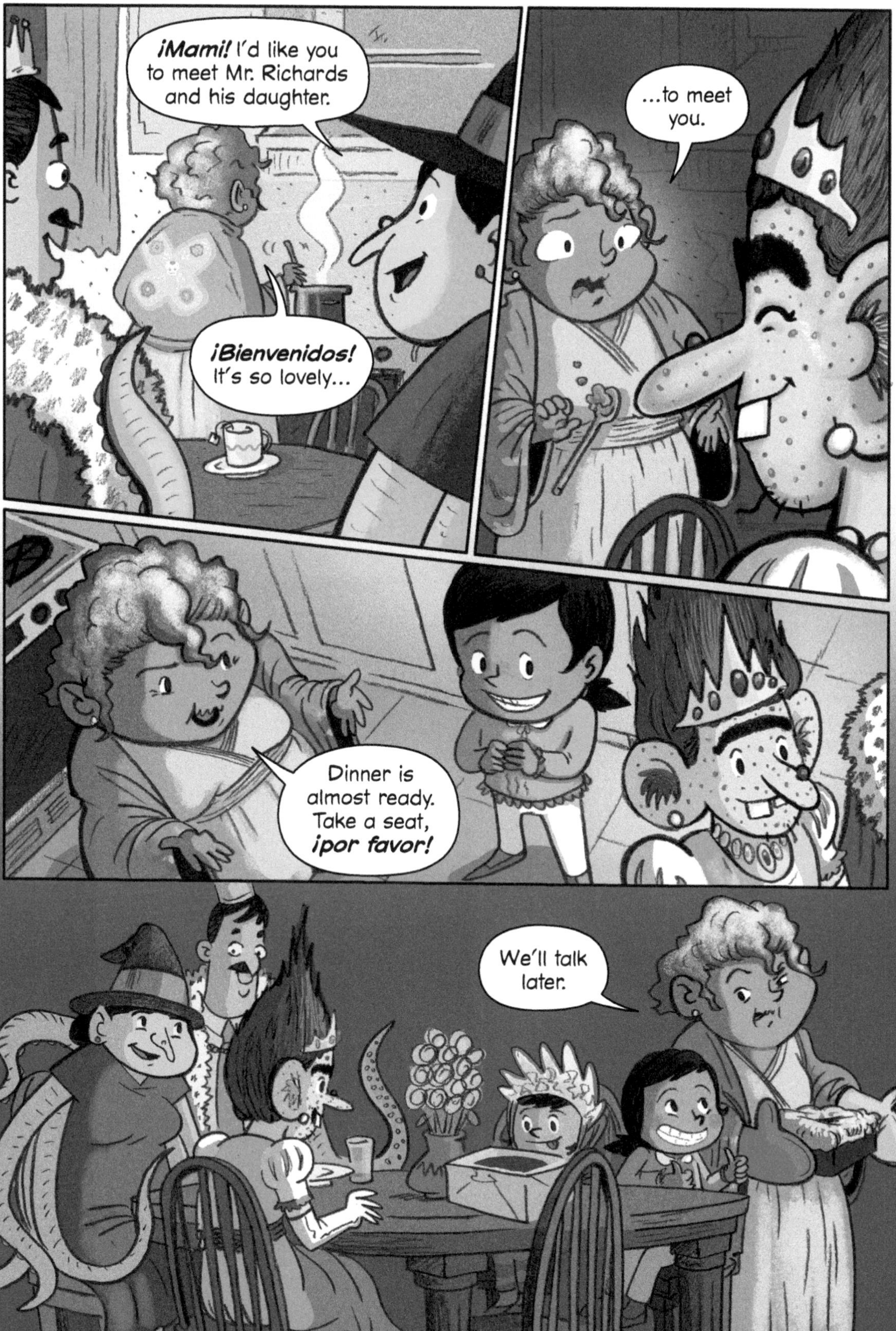
¡Mami! I'd like you to meet Mr. Richards and his daughter.
¡Bienvenidos! It's so lovely...
...to meet you.
Dinner is almost ready. Take a seat, ¡por favor!
We'll talk later.

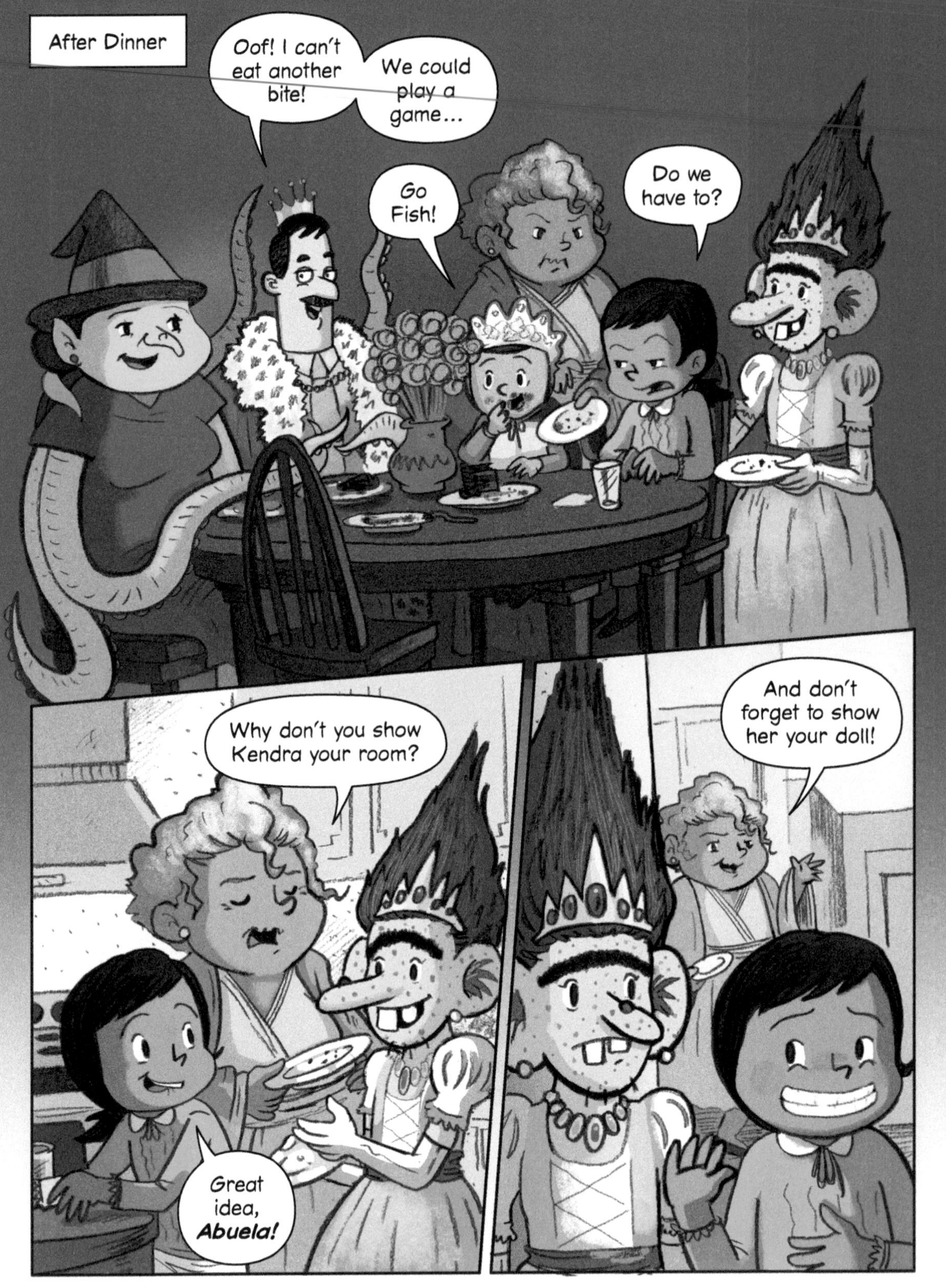
After Dinner
Oof! I can't eat another bite!
We could play a game...
Go Fish!
Do we have to?
Why don't you show Kendra your room?
Great idea, ***Abuela!***
And don't forget to show her your doll!

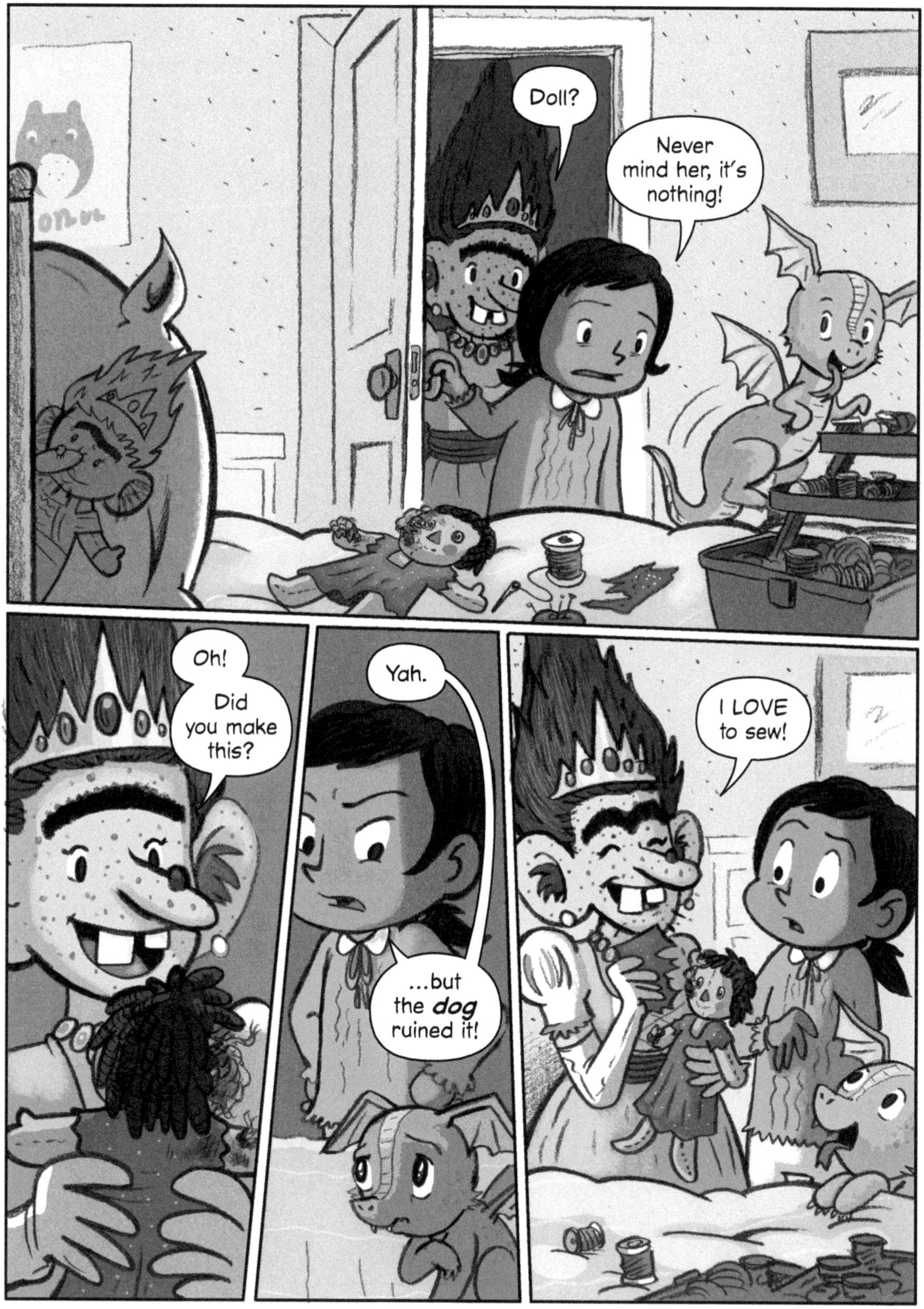
Doll?
Never mind her, it's nothing!
Oh!
Did you make this?
Yah.
...but the *dog* ruined it!
I LOVE to sew!

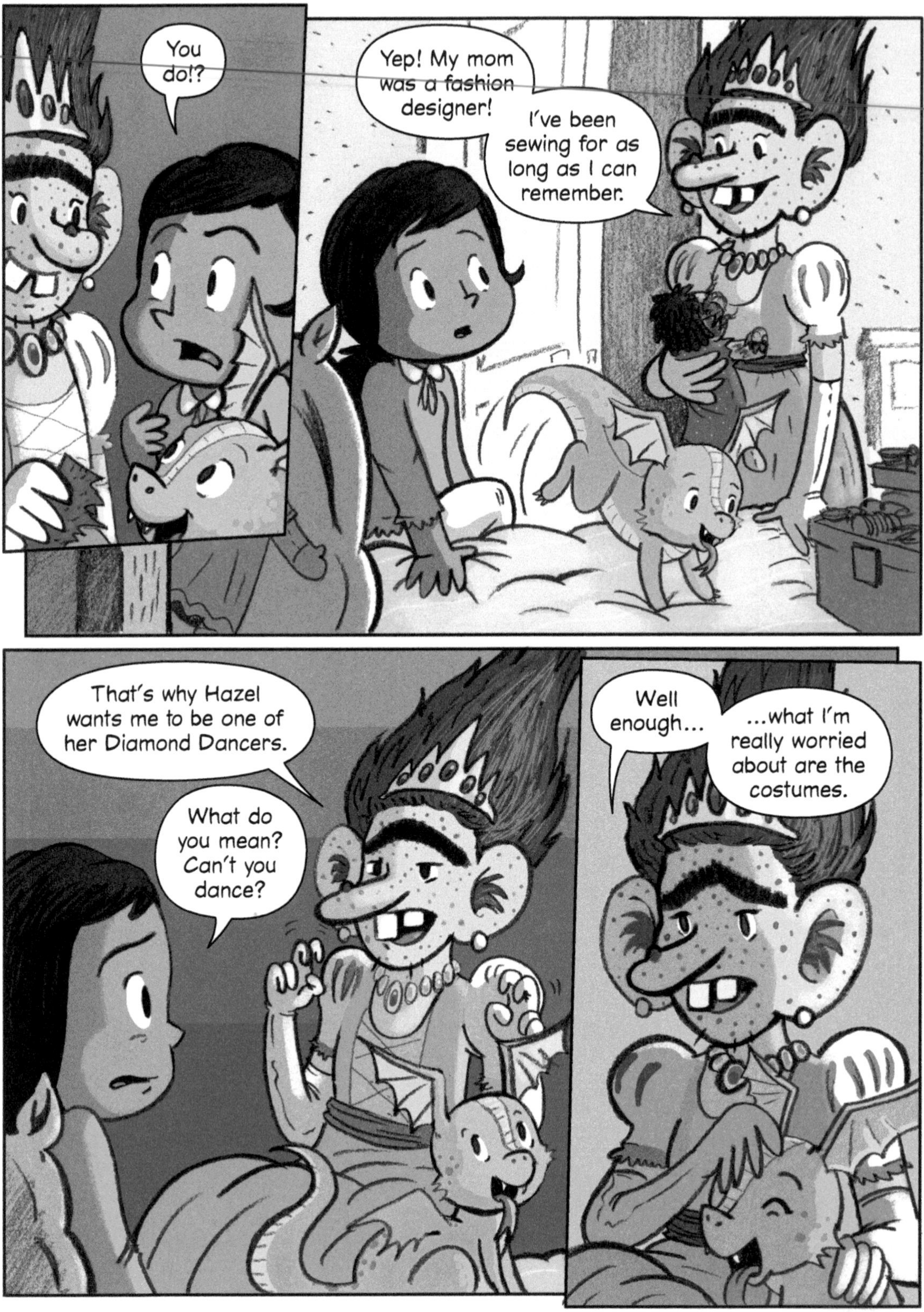
You do!?
Yep! My mom was a fashion designer!
I've been sewing for as long as I can remember.
That's why Hazel wants me to be one of her Diamond Dancers.
What do you mean? Can't you dance?
Well enough...
...what I'm really worried about are the costumes.

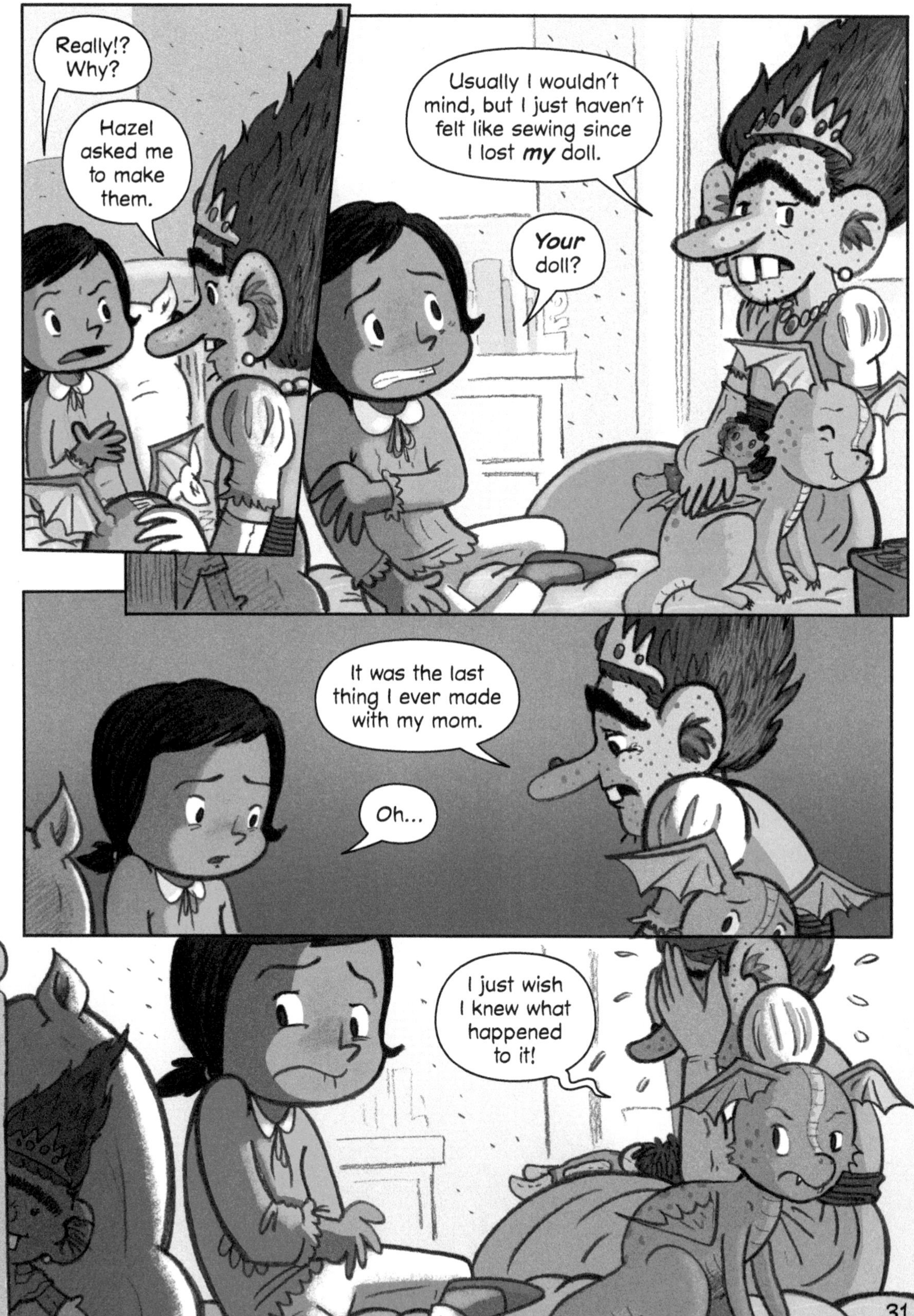
Really!? Why?
Hazel asked me to make them.
Usually I wouldn't mind, but I just haven't felt like sewing since I lost *my* doll.
Your doll?
It was the last thing I ever made with my mom.
Oh...
I just wish I knew what happened to it!

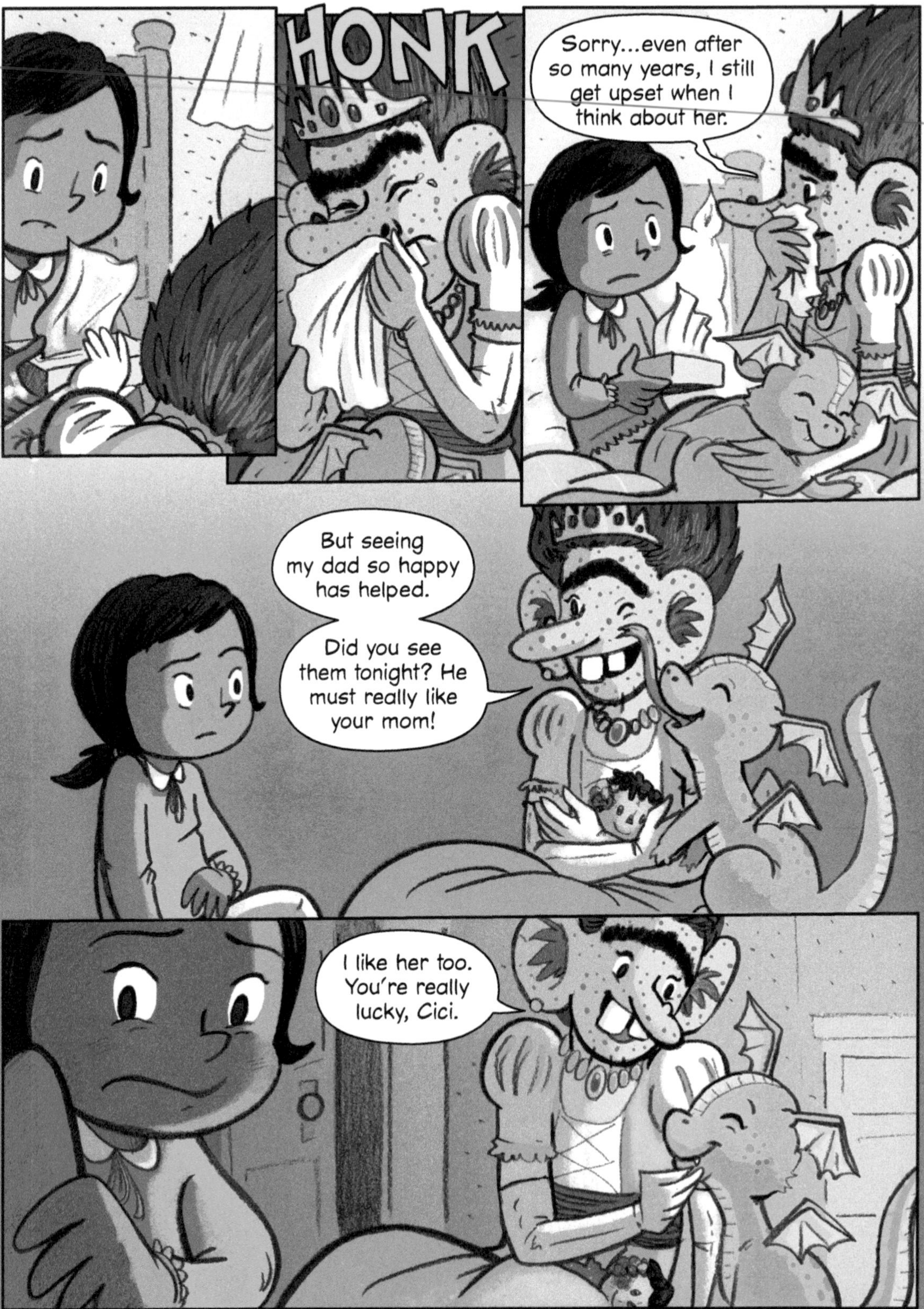
HONK
Sorry...even after so many years, I still get upset when I think about her.
But seeing my dad so happy has helped.
Did you see them tonight? He must really like your mom!
I like her too. You're really lucky, Cici.

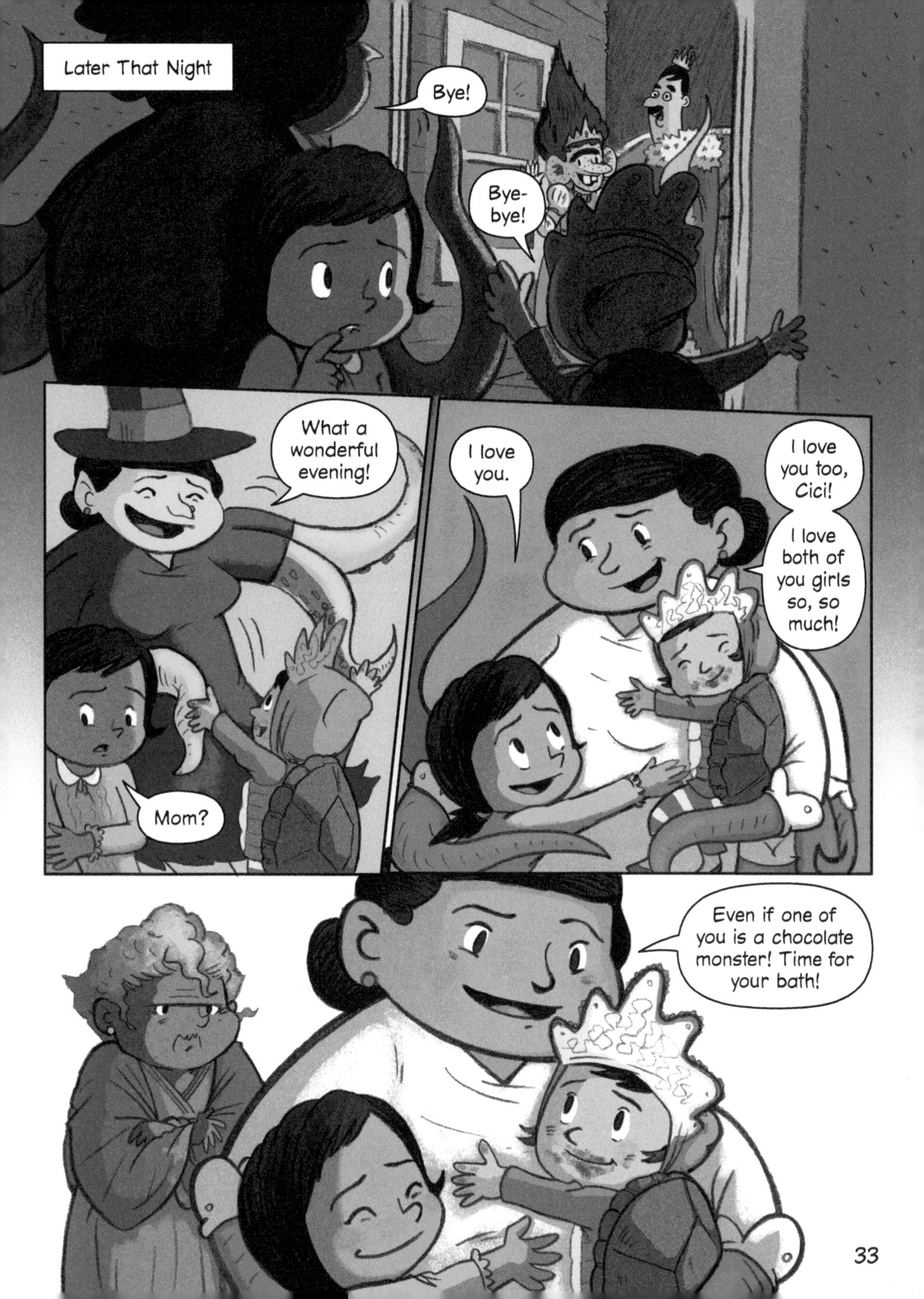
Later That Night
Bye!
Bye-bye!
What a wonderful evening!
Mom?
I love you.
I love you too, Cici!
I love both of you girls so, so much!
Even if one of you is a chocolate monster! Time for your bath!

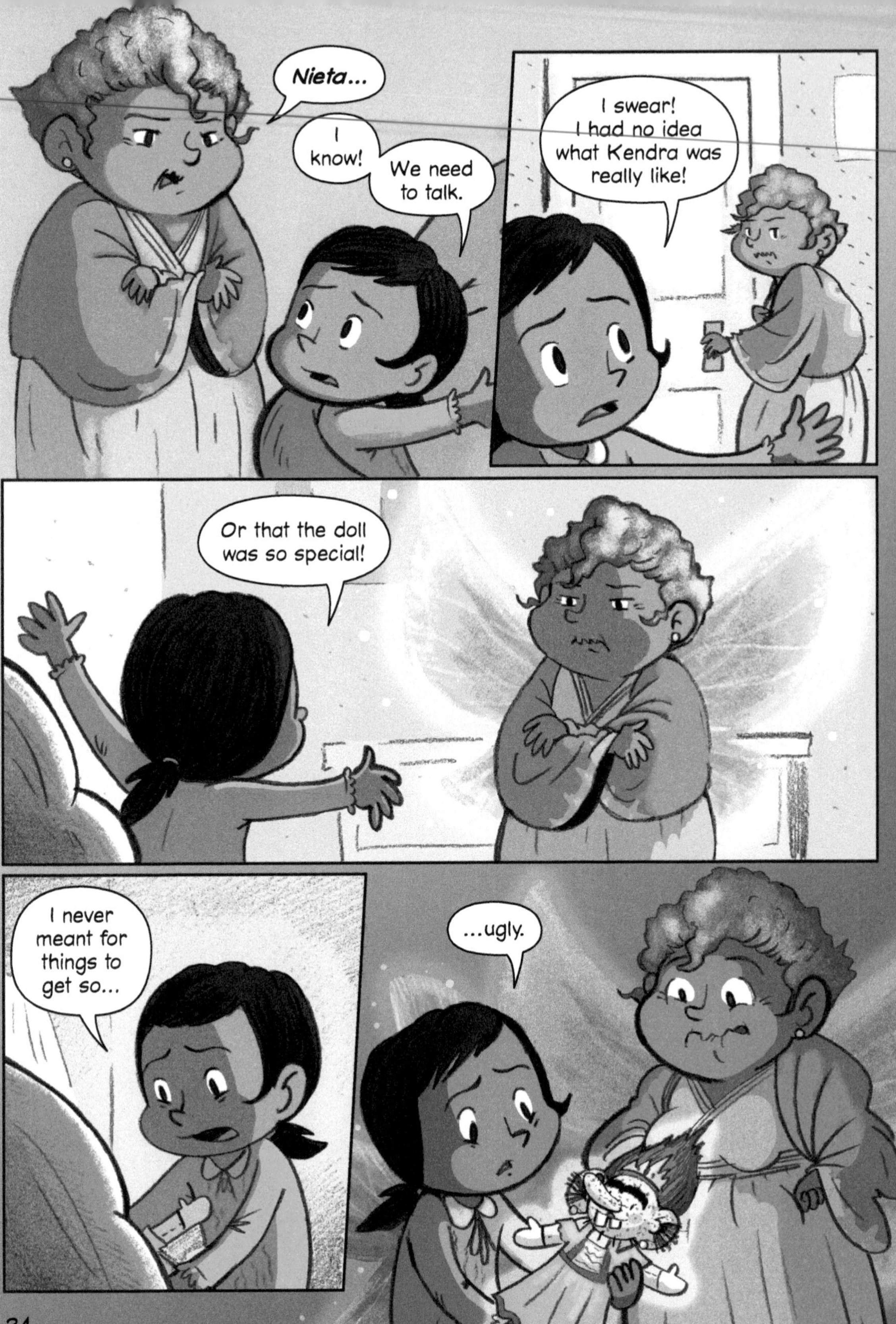
Nieta...
I know!
We need to talk.
I swear! I had no idea what Kendra was really like!
Or that the doll was so special!
I never meant for things to get so...
...ugly.

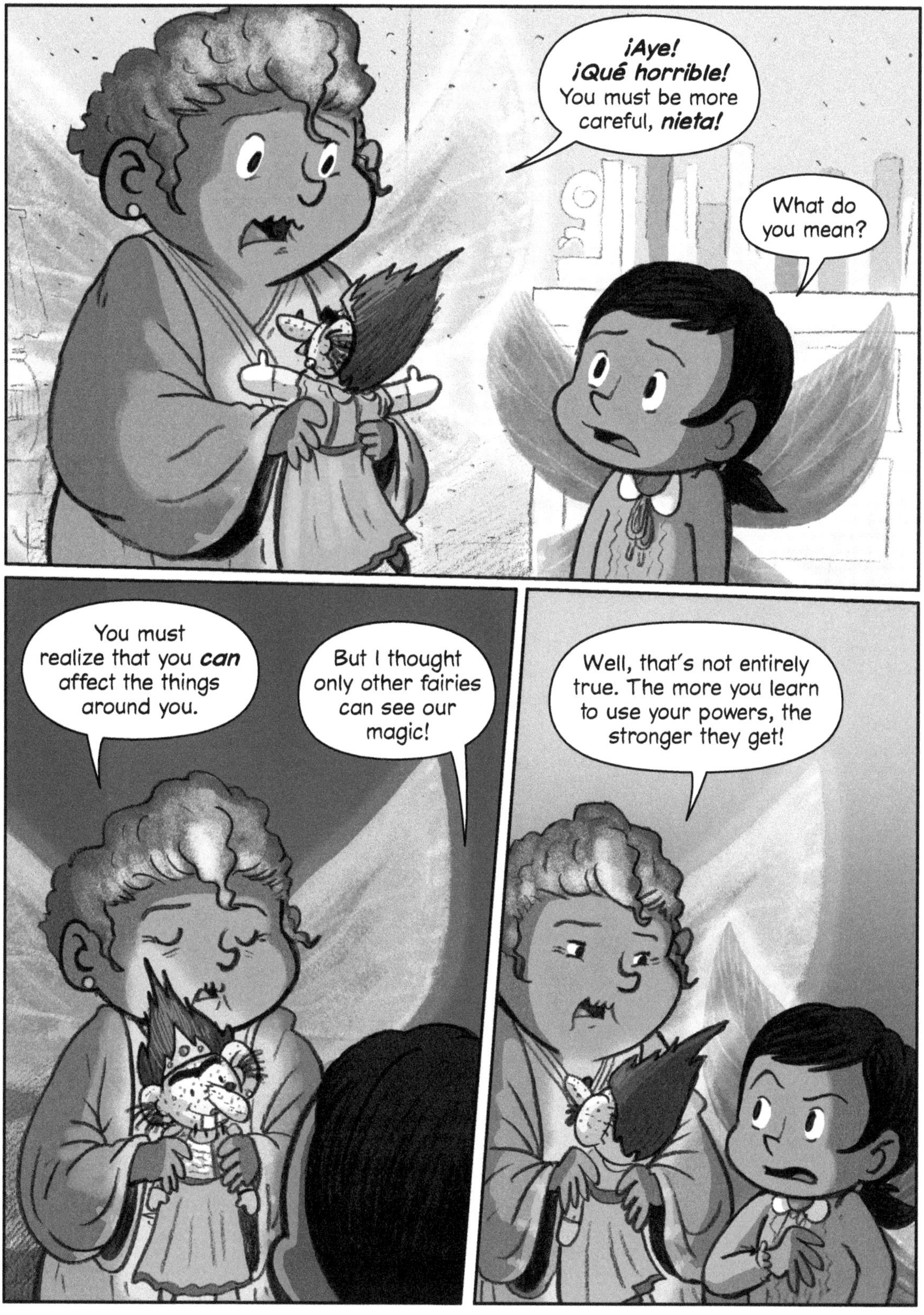
¡Aye! ¡Qué horrible! You must be more careful, nieta!
What do you mean?
You must realize that you can affect the things around you.
But I thought only other fairies can see our magic!
Well, that's not entirely true. The more you learn to use your powers, the stronger they get!

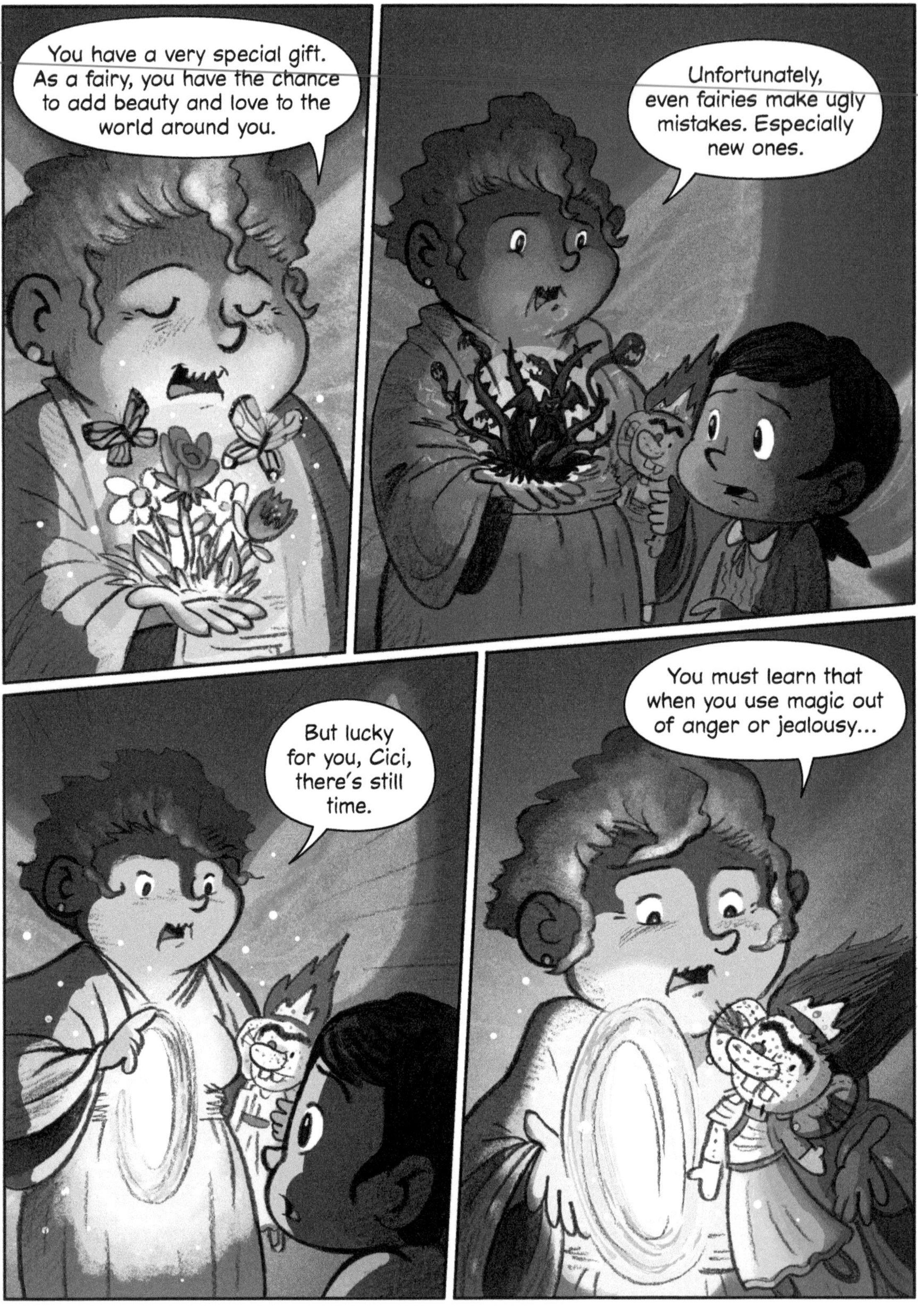
You have a very special gift. As a fairy, you have the chance to add beauty and love to the world around you.
Unfortunately, even fairies make ugly mistakes. Especially new ones.
But lucky for you, Cici, there's still time.
You must learn that when you use magic out of anger or jealousy...

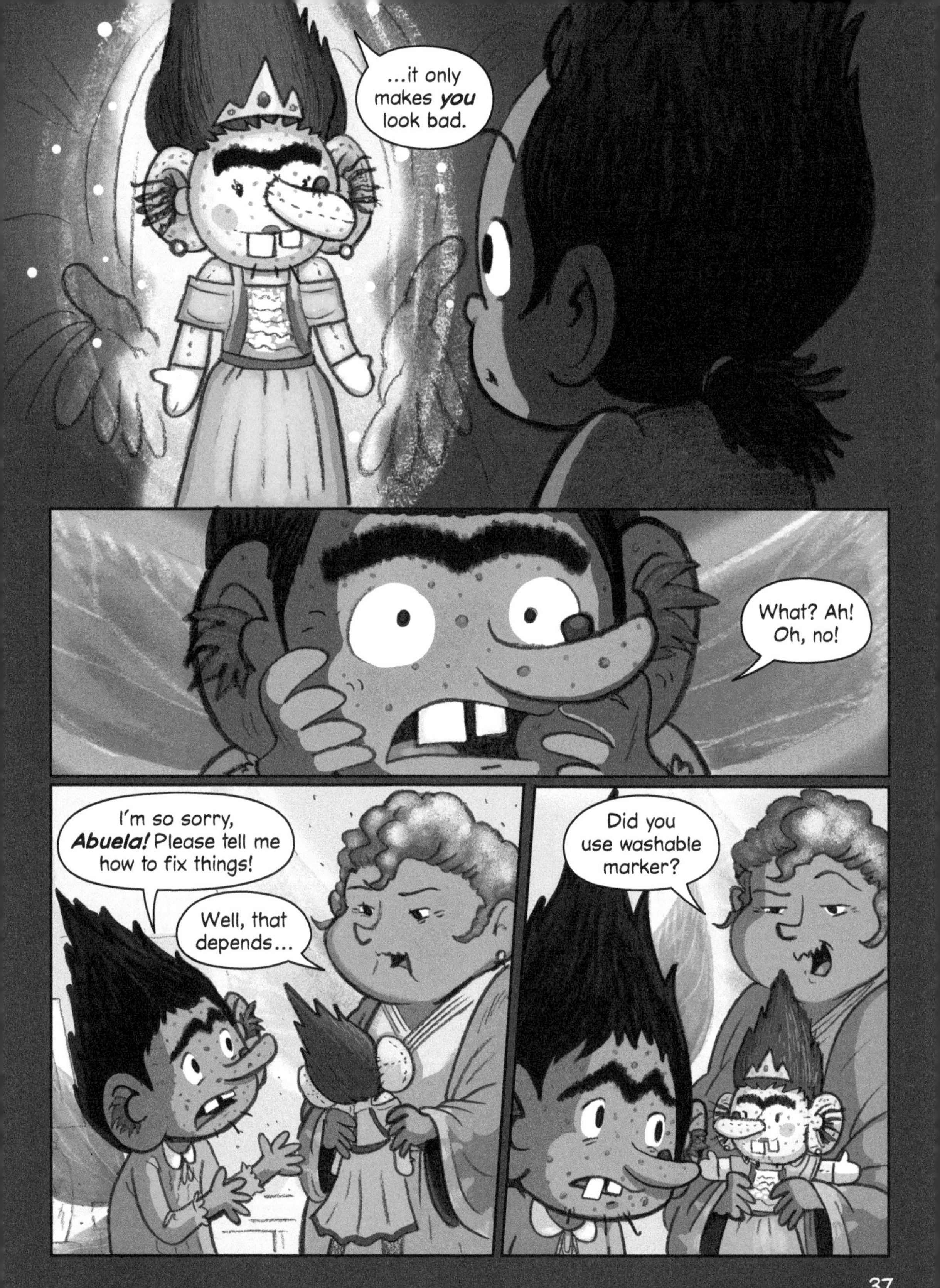

...it only makes ***you*** look bad.
What? Ah! Oh, no!
I'm so sorry, ***Abuela!*** Please tell me how to fix things!
Well, that depends...
Did you use washable marker?

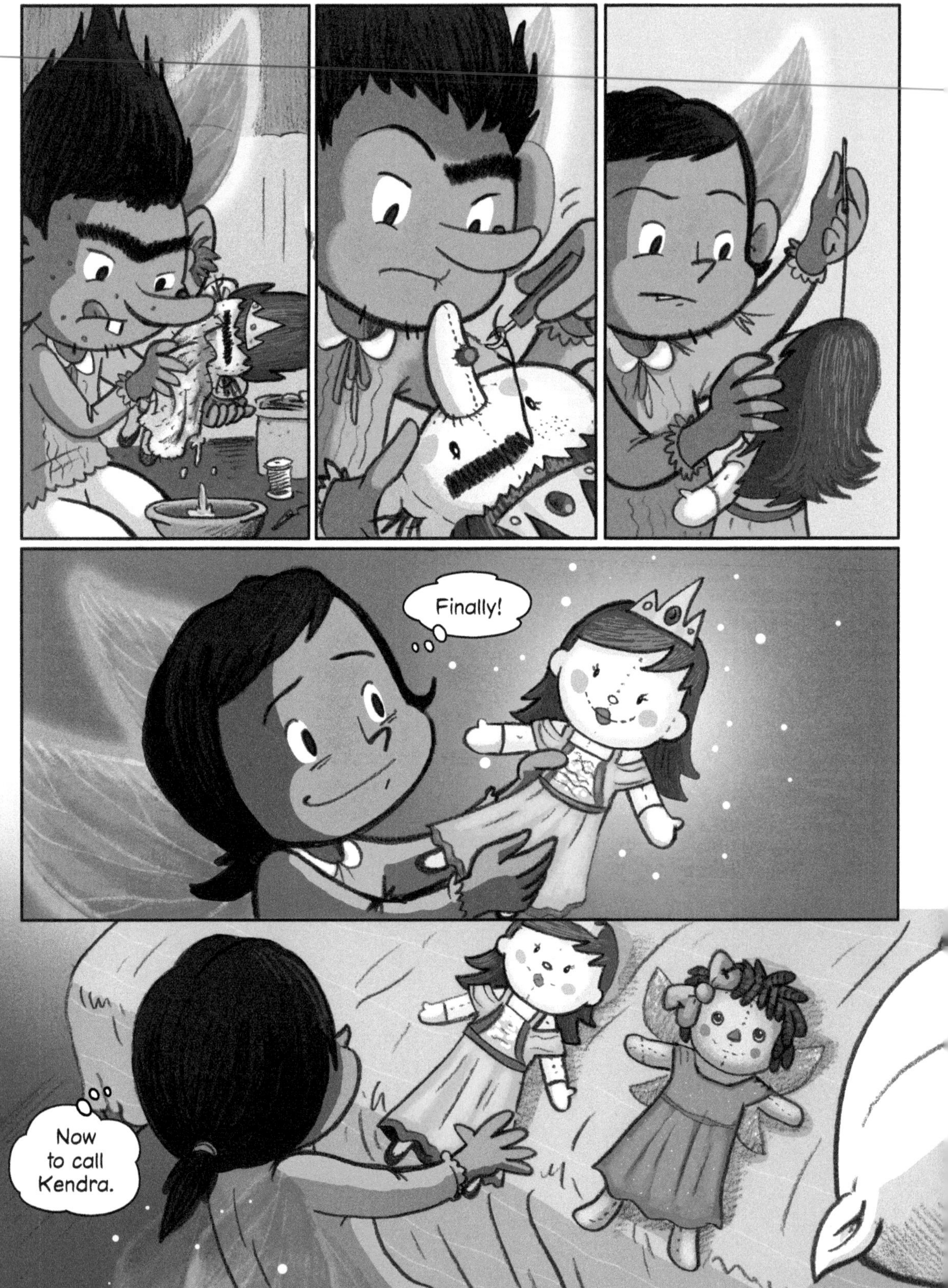
Finally!
Now to call Kendra.

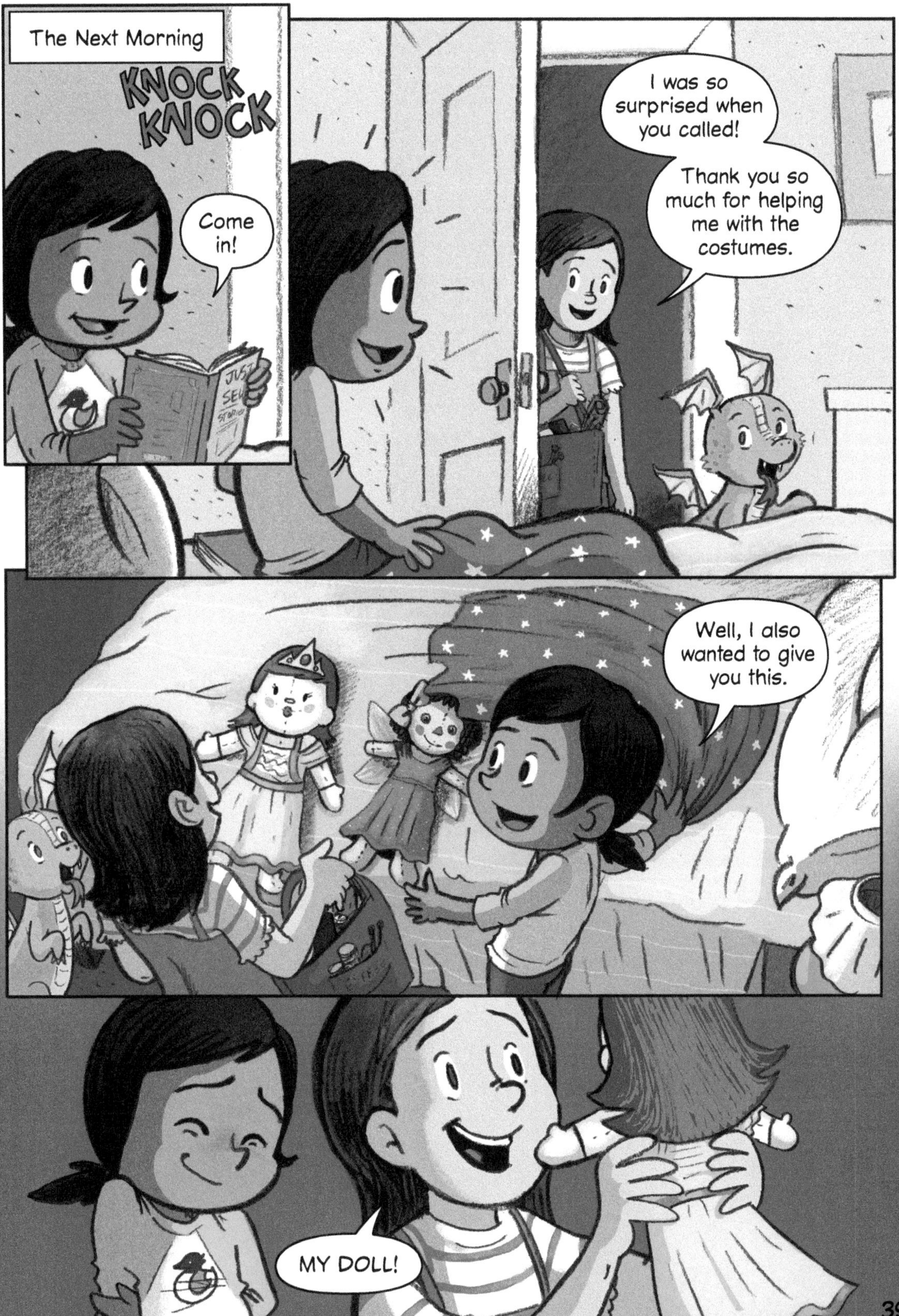
The Next Morning
KNOCK KNOCK
Come in!
JUST SEW STORIES
I was so surprised when you called!
Thank you so much for helping me with the costumes.
Well, I also wanted to give you this.
MY DOLL!

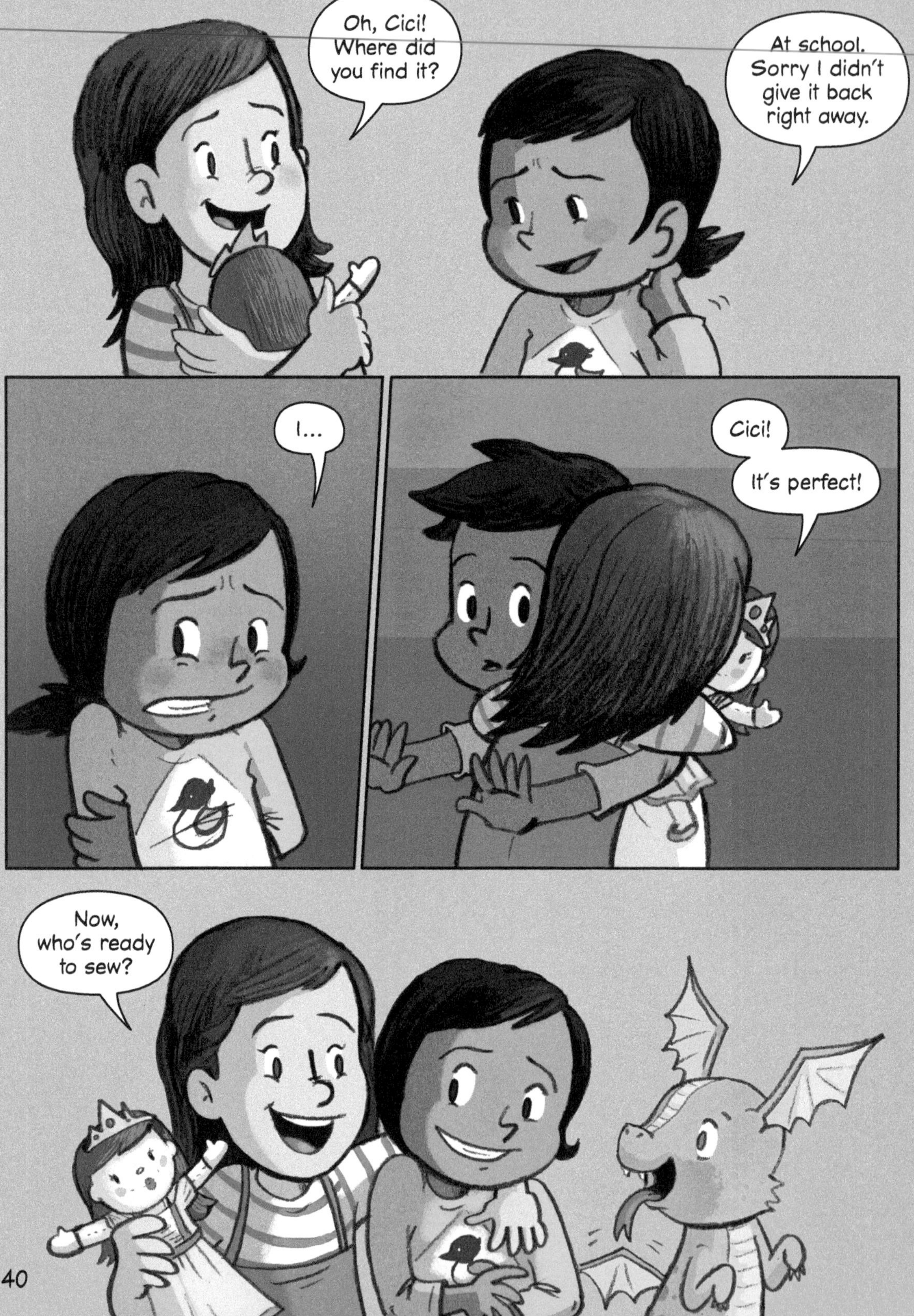
Oh, Cici! Where did you find it?
At school. Sorry I didn't give it back right away.
I...
Cici!
It's perfect!
Now, who's ready to sew?

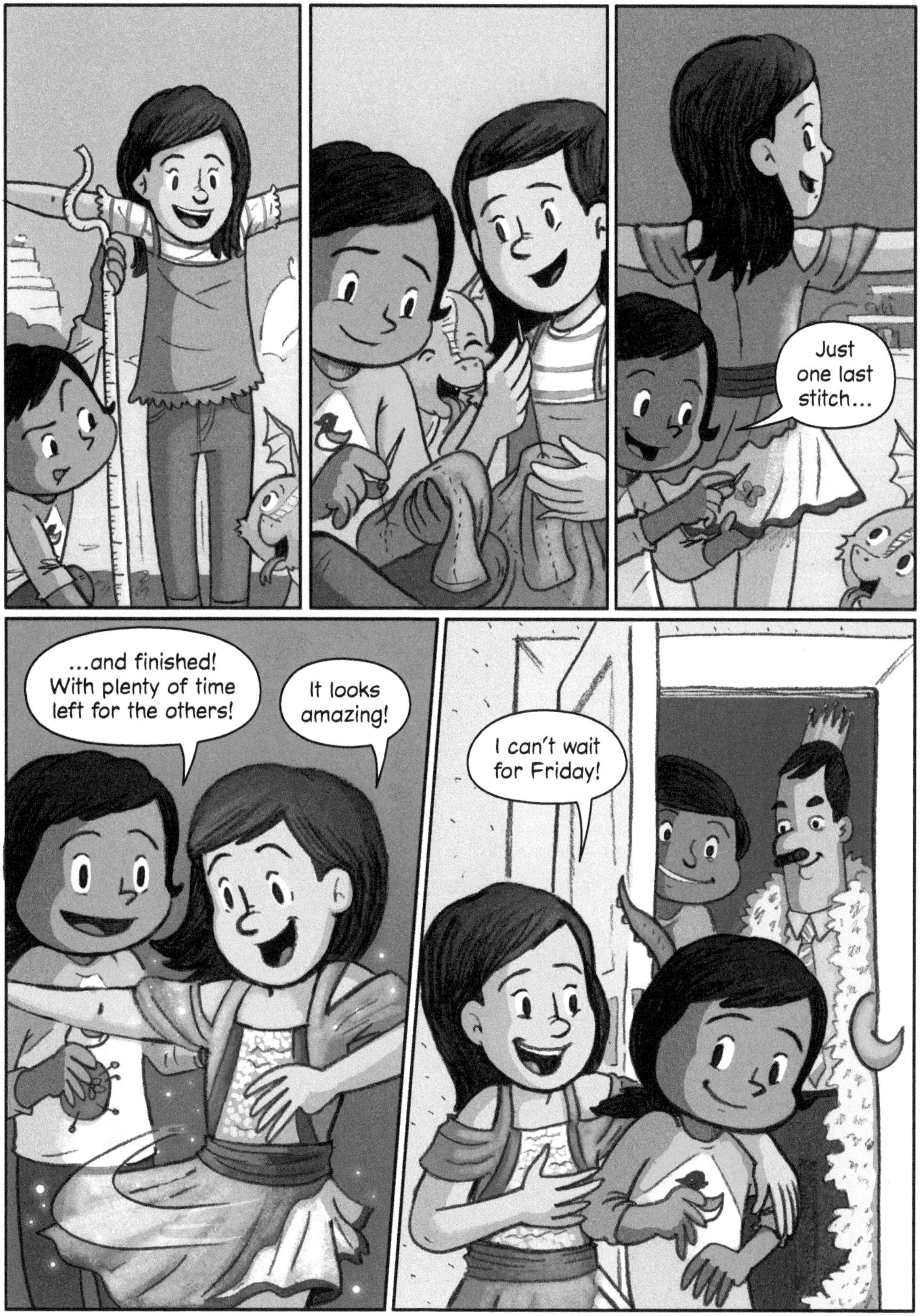
Just one last stitch...
...and finished! With plenty of time left for the others!
It looks amazing!
I can't wait for Friday!

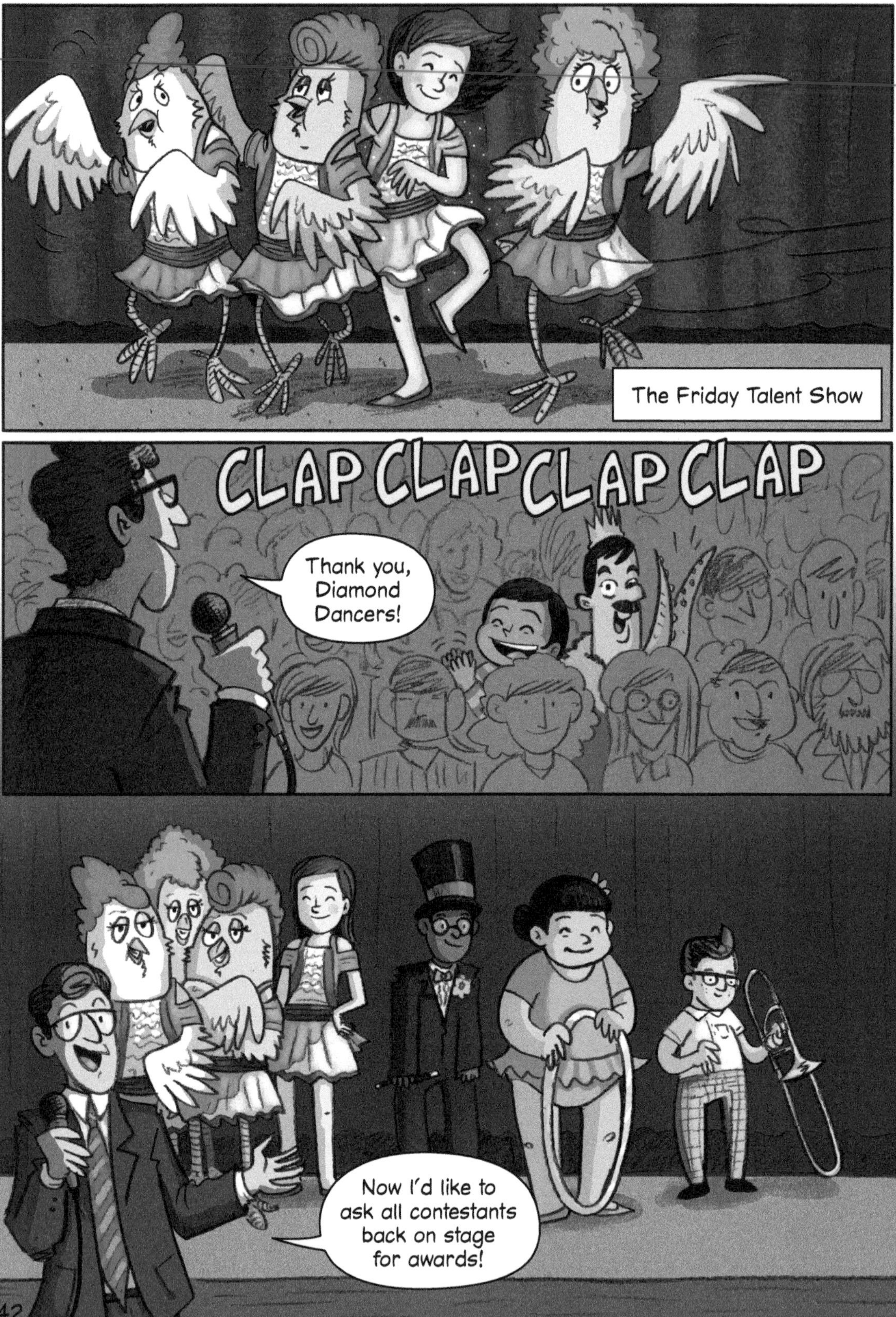
The Friday Talent Show
CLAP CLAP CLAP CLAP
Thank you, Diamond Dancers!
Now I'd like to ask all contestants back on stage for awards!

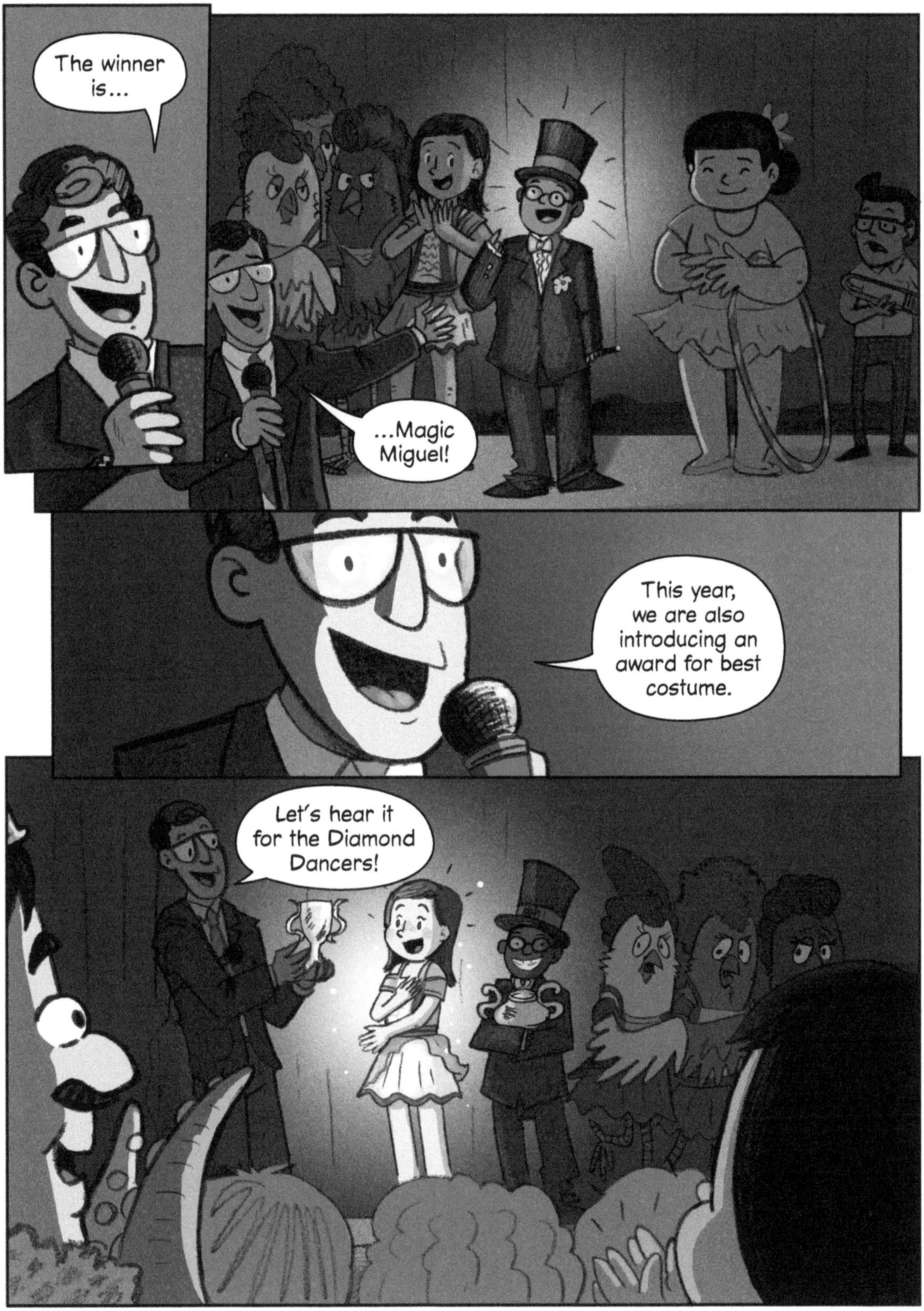
The winner is...
...Magic Miguel!
This year, we are also introducing an award for best costume.
Let's hear it for the Diamond Dancers!

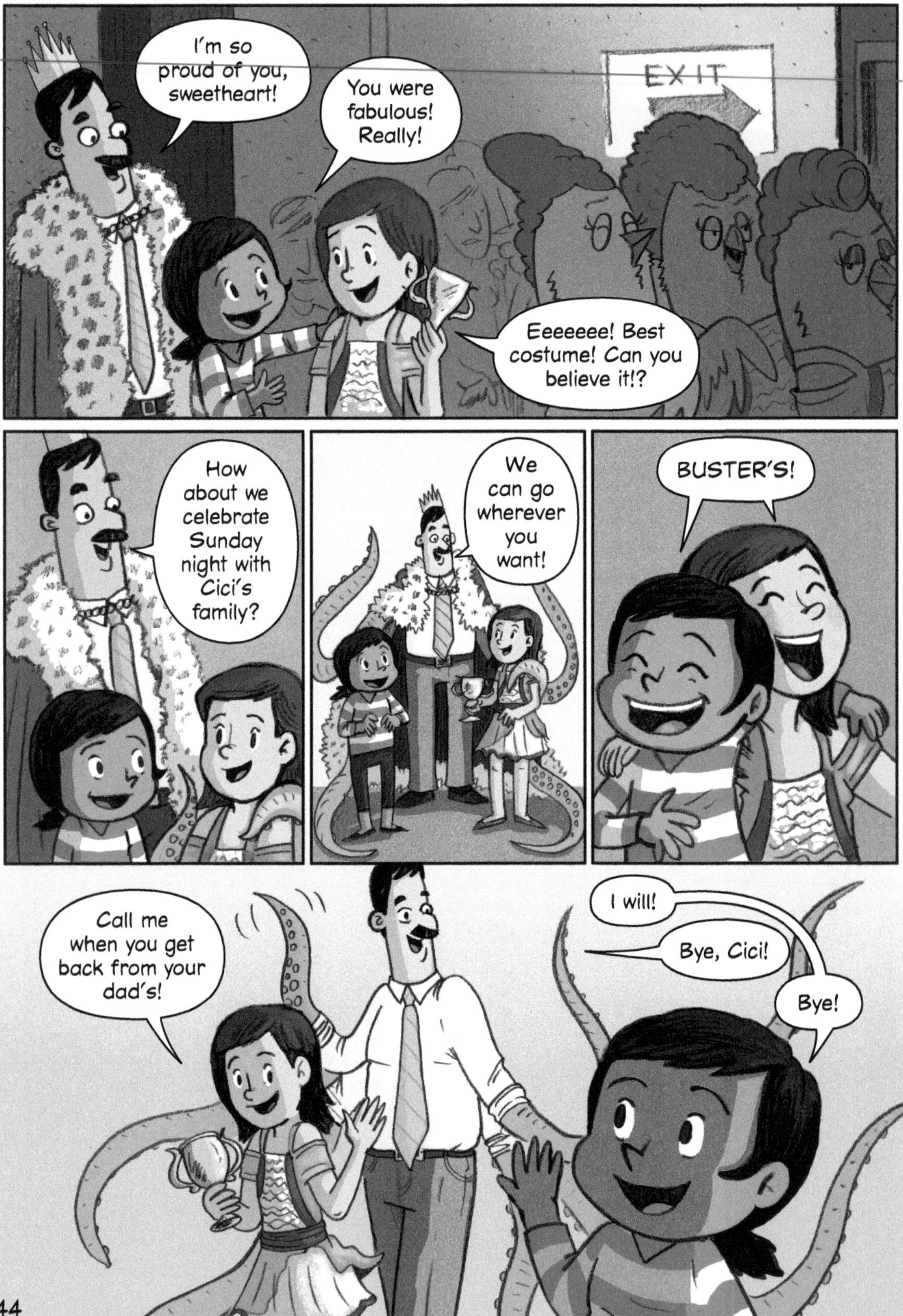
I'm so proud of you, sweetheart!
You were fabulous! Really!
EXIT
Eeeeeee! Best costume! Can you believe it!?
How about we celebrate Sunday night with Cici's family?
We can go wherever you want!
BUSTER'S!
Call me when you get back from your dad's!
I will!
Bye, Cici!
Bye!

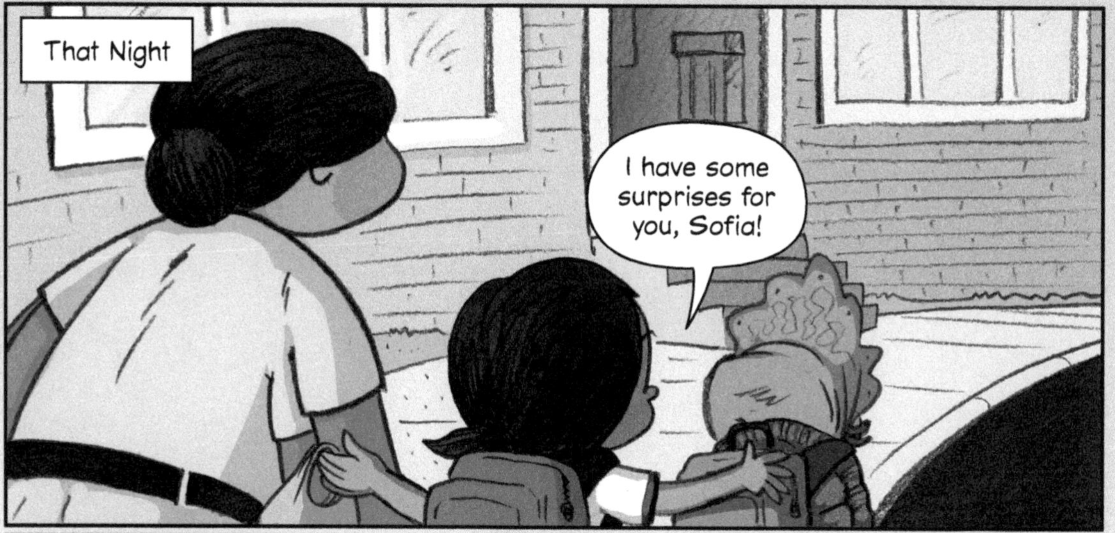
That Night
I have some surprises for you, Sofia!

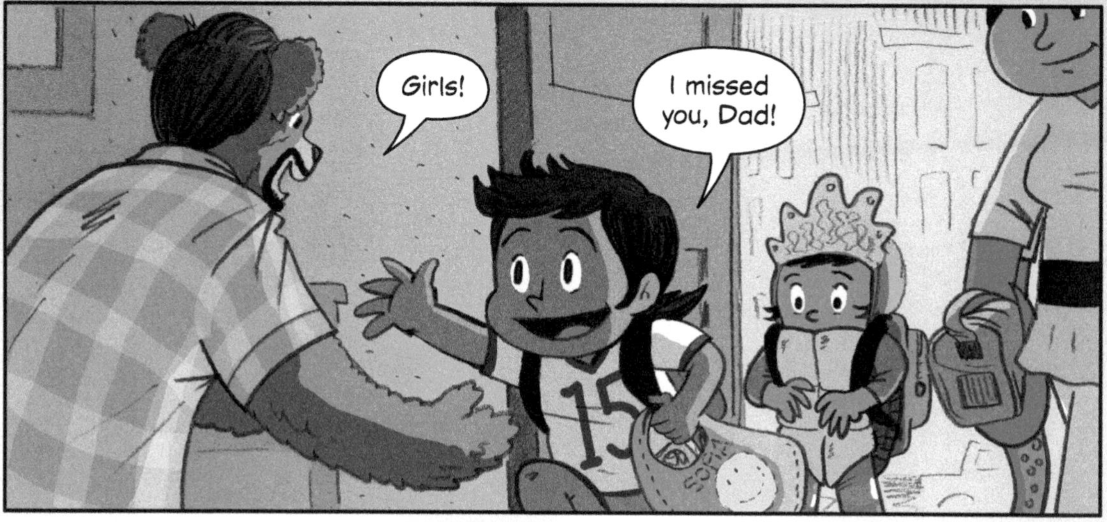
Girls!
I missed you, Dad!

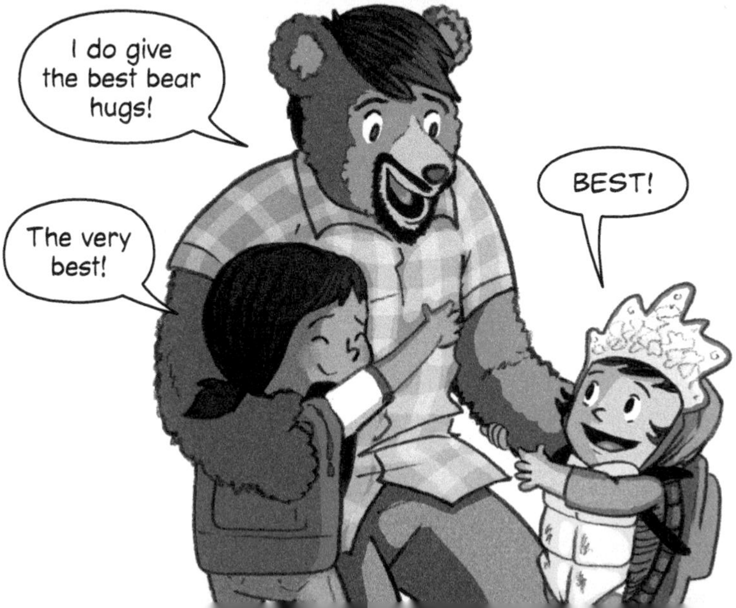
I do give the best bear hugs!
The very best!
BEST!

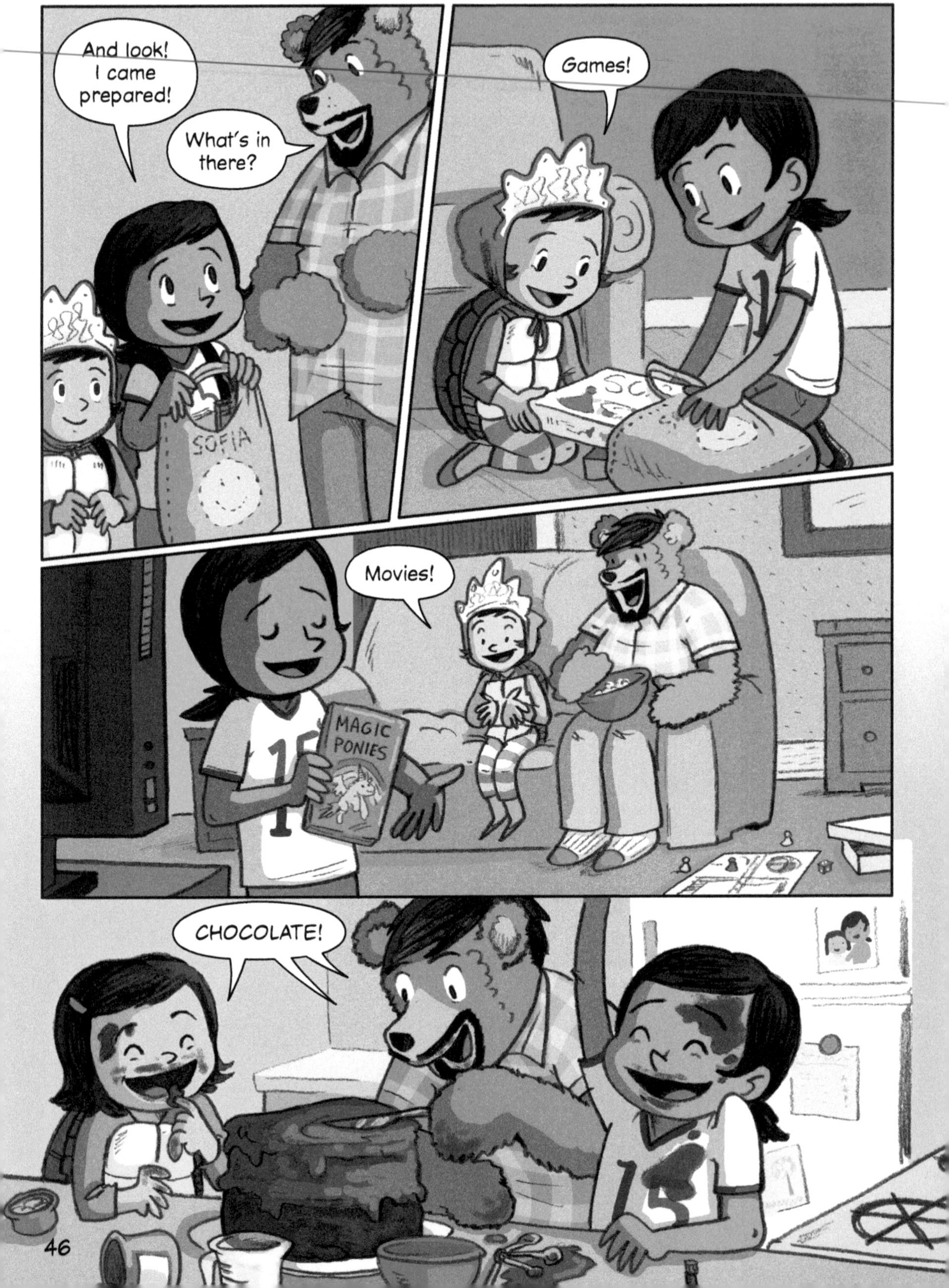
And look! I came prepared!
What's in there?
Games!
Movies!
MAGIC PONIES
CHOCOLATE!

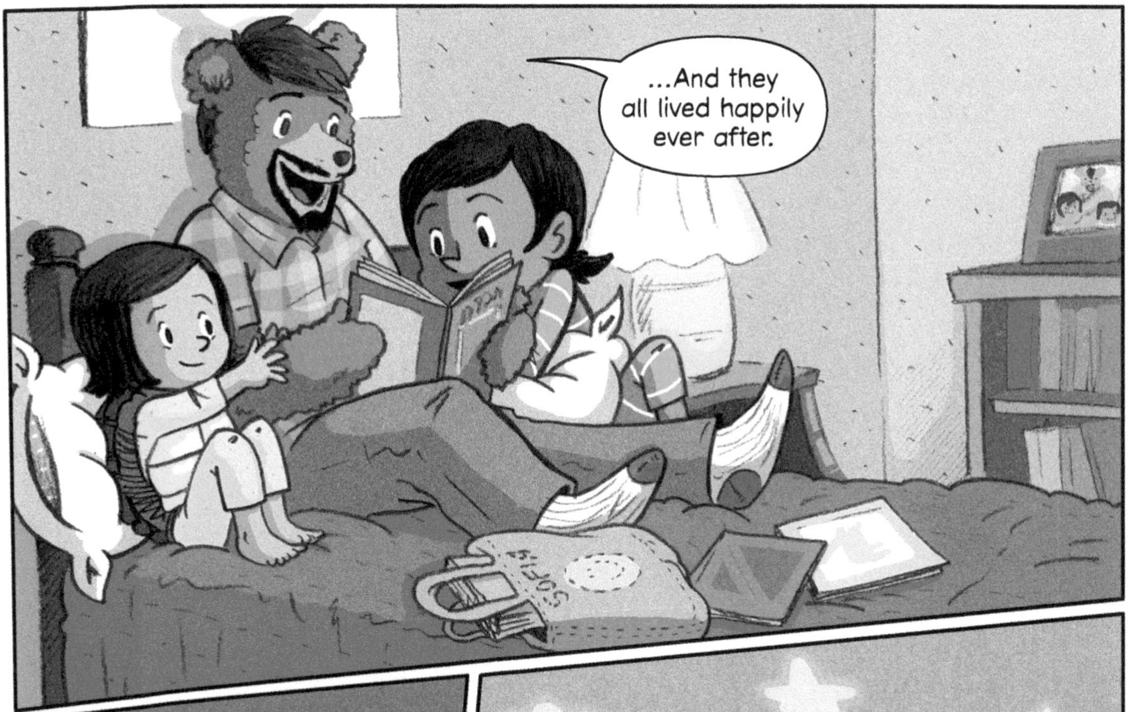
...And they all lived happily ever after.
SOFIA

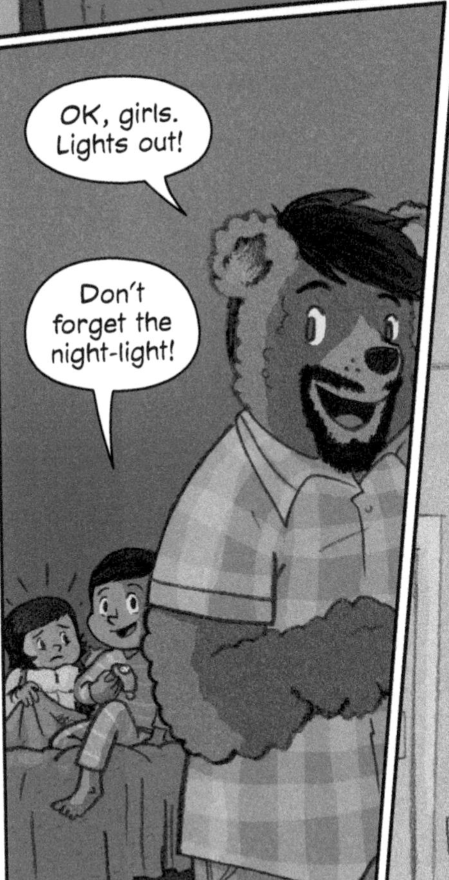
OK, girls. Lights out!
Don't forget the night-light!

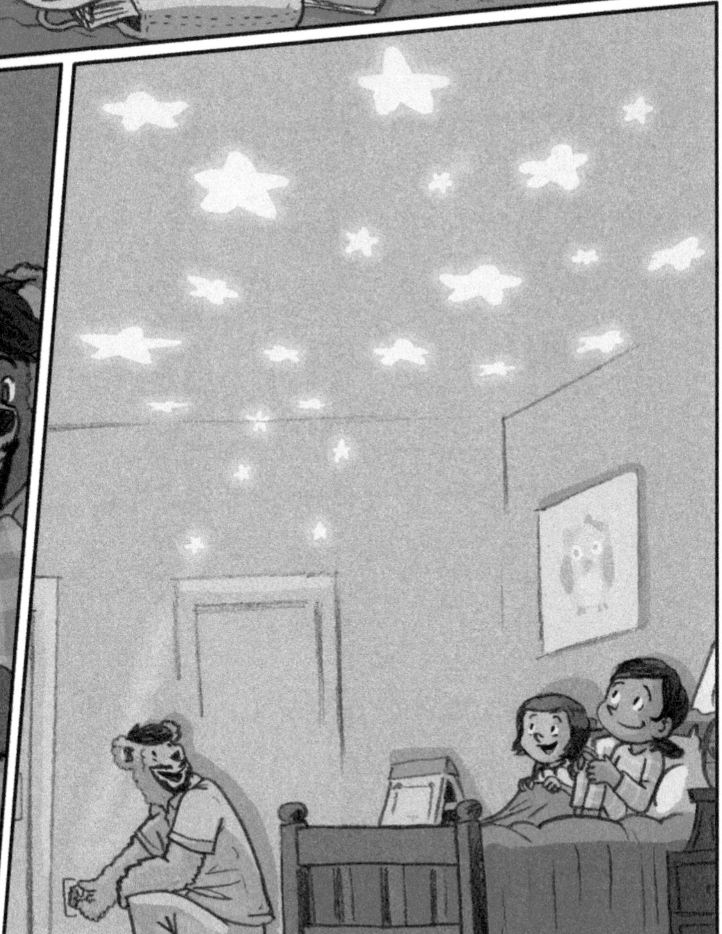

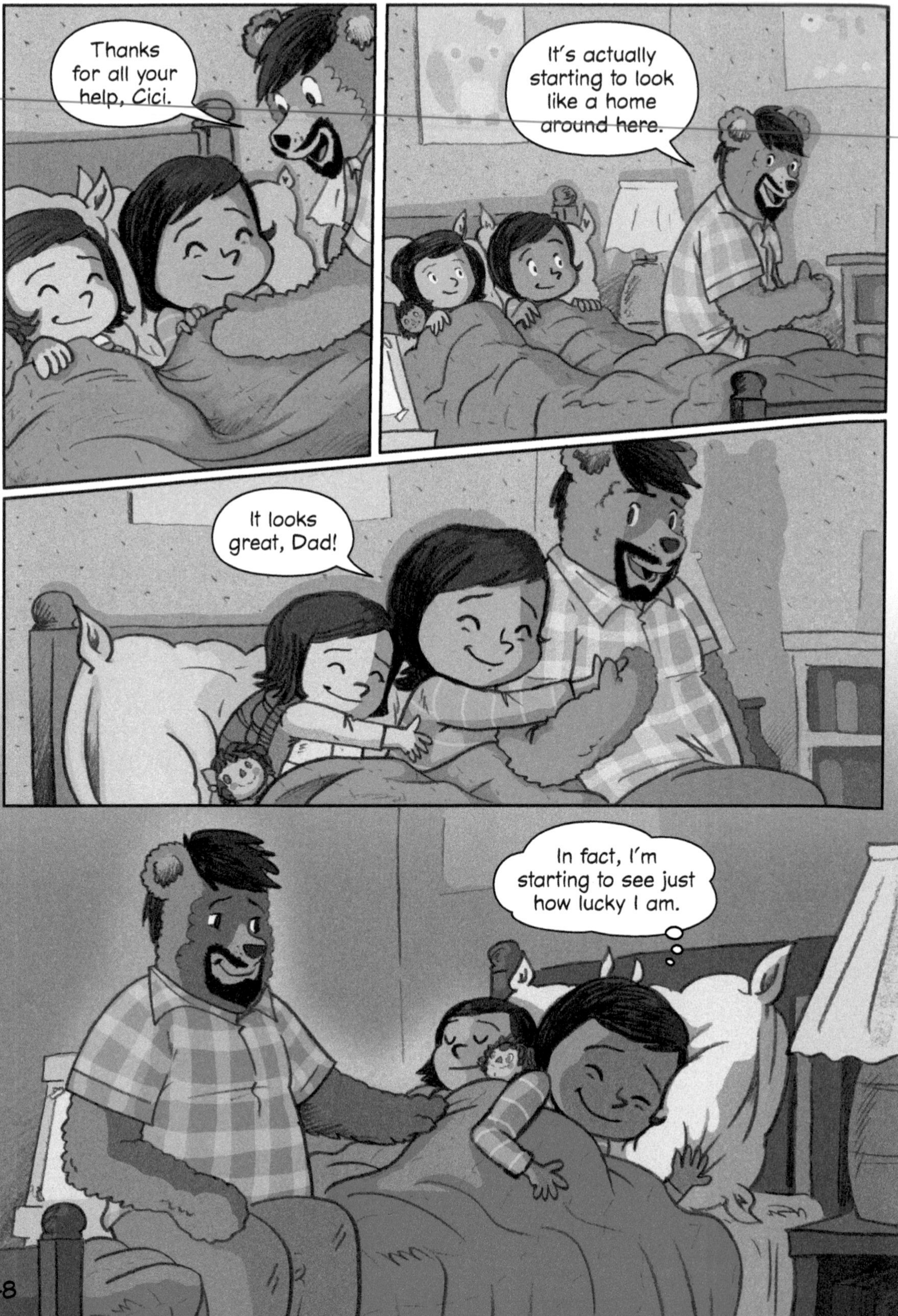
Thanks for all your help, Cici.
It's actually starting to look like a home around here.
It looks great, Dad!
In fact, I'm starting to see just how lucky I am.